SPOTTED HER FIRST

KLAMATH MOUNTAIN PRIDE

EMMA DEAN

SPOTTED HER FIRST

ASIN: B07CZ4HWNW

SPOTTED HER FIRST

CHAPTER ONE

PIPER

Piper checked the spine of the book again and then slid it into place. She sighed and climbed down the ladder carefully. One more hour and she could close the library. Sometimes she regretted taking the night shift, but it was always so much quieter.

Every night at eleven she closed up and went straight home, even on Fridays. Piper didn't have a life outside her research, Cat Solo, and her dance classes. And she preferred it that way. The excitement of history was far more interesting to her than real life.

Libraries were always the quietest on Friday nights. It was actually her favorite time to work. Something about the silence and the books felt almost holy – like a gateway to another universe, or reality. Sometimes when she read about those days in Egypt so, so long ago it felt like it wasn't even real, like those stories were from another planet or perhaps just made up.

The Hellenistic Period had stolen her heart and

Sacramento State had the entire Tsakopoulos Hellenic Collection. It was a strange obsession she'd had ever since her father did one of those spit swab things where you find out your true ancestry.

When she was fifteen years old Piper learned she was descended from Cleopatra VII herself and so began her obsession with Alexander the Great, Ptolemy I, Marc Antony, and Cleopatra.

She checked the remaining books in the cart, mentally checking off what needed to be done before she could leave. Piper pulled the cart along with her and let her mind drift as she so often did. After she'd gotten her Bachelor's in Library Science she'd gone back for a Master's in History, and then finally her PhD. Her thesis was centered on whether Cleopatra truly did kill herself or not – a story told by her conqueror which made it suspicious. But there was just not enough information, not enough proof.

Piper sighed. Maybe she should change her thesis again. Her true interest was the love story between Marc Antony and Cleopatra, but it wasn't something she could really write a thesis on.

No one risked their life for love anymore and that made her melancholy. A 'daydreamer' as her father said. Her dad was the practical and logical one. He was always reminding her that real life had to be dealt with whether she liked it or not.

It was because of him she owned a gun. Having a cop dad had never made her dating life easy, but Piper didn't care. Her dad was better than any stupid guy. Whenever she had the urge to date again it was quickly squashed by some dumb frat boy testing her patience.

The doors to the library swung wide open and Piper

jumped at the sudden sound. She checked her watch with a frown. No one came in this late on a Friday night.

"Are you sure this is the right place?" someone asked. He sounded...like velvet and brandy.

It was the stupidest thought Piper had ever had in her life and she'd certainly had some doozies. But there was no better way to describe the soft male voice that seemed to drift through her library like smoke.

"The witch said it was," another man said. These voices were definitely not the boys she was used to. They were deep, gruff, and somehow sensual.

Piper frowned at the word 'witch.' Moving silently through the stacks Piper positioned herself so she could see who was in her library so late at night.

"I'm going to find her first," one taunted.

"Oh no you aren't, I am."

"You're mistaken if you think either of you are faster than me."

What the heck were they talking about? Whatever it was she didn't like the sound of it. Either they were searching for one of the students...or her. Neither sounded very safe. Piper cursed herself for being so far from her desk and the taser she kept in her purse.

Slowly she moved deeper into the shadowy stacks, keeping to the back. She just wanted to get out of the library without any confrontation. She didn't know what these guys had planned, but she wasn't stupid enough to wait and find out.

At least there were multiple exits. Piper pulled her phone out of her pocket and made sure it was on silent. She could text security but her dad would be there faster. She sent off a quick text and asked him to come to the library. It was difficult to ask him to come pick her up early without setting off his panic. But his patrol was in her area. It was the safest way.

Piper may not have anything on her person to defend herself with, but her dad had always said *anything* could be a weapon. She grabbed the heaviest book she could find in hardback. It wouldn't do much but it would disorient an attacker.

So many years of self-defense classes and days at the gun range that she'd absolutely hated. Her father had insisted. Piper had never been so grateful for Dad's bullheaded insistence in her life.

The voices stopped suddenly and Piper went still, cocking her head to try and figure out where the men had gone off to. The library was massive. They could be anywhere.

"Spotted her first, boys. I win," a deep, rolling voice said from directly behind her.

Piper gasped and whirled around. The man before her was definitely like no one she'd ever seen before. Well, not in real life. He looked like he should be a model with his jade-green eyes and tanned skin. His blond-brown hair was thick and gorgeous, but it was his *presence* that had her captivated.

Then her senses came back to her. Piper hurled the book at his face as hard as she could and let out a little screech.

So much for leaving without them noticing, and they were *definitely* looking for *her*.

Piper took off running. It was difficult to keep tabs on them while she ran blindly through the library stacks for the exit. She looked over her shoulder and then slammed into something rock hard.

"Careful there," one of those seductive voices told her.

Piper looked up into the most beautiful brown eyes she'd ever seen. They were light brown and had a bit of red in them, like amber. His teeth were white against his dark skin when he smiled at her, but it did nothing to relieve her fear.

She didn't know what these men wanted with her, but there were three of them and only one of her. And they were huge. It would be best to ask questions later – preferably with other people around. Her heart pounded in her chest and despite how mesmerized by him she was – her instinct to flee was stronger. She brought her knee up into his groin without even thinking.

Instantly the man released her with a curse and she took off.

Piper ducked down another row, but another man with ice blue eyes and blond hair stared at her like he knew exactly where she'd planned to go. She was frozen in place as she stared at him. He was too beautiful to be real, but the way he walked towards her...this man had the same presence as the other two. It was more of a prowl than a walk and it left her weak in the knees and breathless.

The way she was attracted to them made absolutely no sense to her. Piper wanted to stop and get to know them, but that more than anything was what scared her. When was the last time she wanted to talk to any guy, let alone three? It felt like a trap.

The blond man moved toward her and Piper grabbed every book her hands touched and hurled them at him, screeching and generally making as much noise as she could. Maybe someone would hear her and come see what all the racket was about.

Piper had heard the horror stories before about rapes and such. She refused to be another victim.

"Christ woman, would you stop?" he yelled.

"We're not here to hurt you," another yelled from somewhere within the library stacks.

They may be telling the truth but Piper was done. This was too weird.

She ran in a different direction. Her purse didn't matter. A taser wouldn't work on all three of them, not in time. She ran as fast as her legs could carry her until she hit one of the exits, listening as the three men behind her cursed and pounded after her.

Someone in a security uniform grabbed her before she hit the opposite wall. "Miss, are you all right?"

Piper shoved her hair from her face and tried to get enough breath to talk. "Yeah I'm fine," she gasped, trying to catch her breath. She pointed back at the library. "There are three guys following me though and I don't know what they want."

The security guard frowned and pulled her with him. "I'll take you somewhere safe and then I'll call in back up."

She nodded numbly. Piper prayed her dad would be there soon. She didn't want to hear his mouth about the hours she kept, but she wanted to see him. Her dad always made her feel safe even if it was just her overactive imagination.

"Hey!"

Piper's heart leapt into her throat when she heard one of those men. She whirled around and hid behind the security guard who refused to let go of her.

"Sir, I'm going to have to ask you to vacate the premises," the security guard said. "Or I'm going to call the cops."

The other two popped out of the library next and Piper squeaked. All three of them were huge and muscled. Definitely not the average Sac State college boys.

All three of them froze when they saw the security guard. Piper watched them sniff the air and she frowned. These guys were so strange. Thank goodness she'd found someone who could help her.

"Get away from her," the green-eyed one growled.

Piper took another step back. It looked like a fight was about to start and she wanted no part of it, but the security guard wouldn't release her. "Please, I just want to get out of here."

Instead of removing his hand from her wrist it tightened painfully and a flash of fear went through her.

"Piper..." the drop-dead gorgeous African American man warned. His voice was so deep she imagined she could feel the vibration of it in the air. "If you can get over here, we'll help you."

She shook her head, not understanding how these strange men could possibly know her name or why the security guard was now somehow the one she should be afraid of. But she felt it – something primal and insistent. Piper had to get *away* from him.

It was difficult to think while she was panicking. What the heck had she even learned in all those classes? Vulnerable locations, right? She glanced back at the three men and every single one of them was tense as they tried to slowly approach. The blond gave her an encouraging nod and for whatever reason it helped.

Piper looked back up at the security guard and he glared at her, expecting *something* from her no doubt. He pulled her close and she hated the feel of his body against hers. His arm went across her chest and he started backing them up. Piper. Wanted. Him. Off.

So she sank her teeth into his arm as hard as she could and bit down until she could taste blood. It was oddly spicy, but she didn't let herself think about it as the guard howled and thrashed. When she hit bone he released her and she ran straight towards the men she'd just run from.

It may have been sheer stupidity, but instincts were telling her if nothing else – they would protect her from the security guard.

"Good girl," the green-eyed hottie murmured, but she ran from him too.

Her dad should be right outside in the parking lot any minute now. Piper knew and trusted her dad, not these guys. She burst through the doors and ran around the fountain. Her eyes searched the area for her dad, but it didn't look like he was there yet.

She ran towards the closest parking lot and then with a loud 'pop' the security guard was suddenly in front of her. Piper gasped and stumbled backward, not quite believing what her eyes were seeing.

"Piper!" her father's familiar voice shouted from farther away than she preferred at the moment.

"Dad!" She turned to run through the quad instead. Piper was officially terrified. This guard could just teleport?

Another 'pop' and the guard was even closer this time. He wrapped his hand around her wrist and she screamed, trying to give anyone her location. The three men shouted her name and Piper glanced over her shoulder to see them coming at her and the guard from three different angles, closing in like hunters.

"I'm sorry," the security guy told her with a grimace. "I didn't want to do this."

And with another 'pop' the world disappeared into inky blackness.

CHAPTER TWO

CALEB

"I told you two to keep an eye on her," he snapped, swiping his hand through his hair and cutting his pride mates a scathing look. "Now that stupid fucking demon has her."

"Look Caleb, the demon can teleport," Niko reminded him – as if they hadn't all seen it for themselves. "Not much I can do about that."

"It didn't help the whole damn library was covered in her scent," Xavier growled. "It made it almost impossible to track her."

Caleb snarled. Even if they were right he didn't have to like it. "How the fuck are we going to find her now? Can you call that crazy witch back?" he asked Niko – who was always the calm one between the three of them.

"I can but I'd keep anything about her being crazy to yourself. Don't even think it. You don't know exactly what these witches are capable of." Niko shot him a glare, mouthy for one of the more submissive members of the pride.

Niko wasn't a sub. He was more...a beta to Xavier and

Caleb's alpha tendencies. He balanced their volatile personalities.

Xavier paced in front of the library, glancing at the man Piper called father. "We need to do something about him. He just saw something pop out of existence with his daughter. It's cruel to leave him like this."

Caleb crossed his arms over his chest. He wasn't going anywhere until he heard what that witch had to say.

"Fine," Xavier snapped. "I'll deal with it."

It was difficult not to throw an insult after the other male. The three of them hadn't really been friends before they'd gotten the call that had spurred them into action. Mates were rare enough the pride had the help of witches to find them. Cat shifters weren't like the wolves. Females didn't mate with only one male.

Caleb didn't know if it was genetics or the magic that allowed them to shapeshift in the first place, but that was just the way it was. The only exception was the fox shifters. Their strange mix of cat and dog allowed the female to mate with more than one or just one. It was up to fate at that point.

Thank the gods the witches were neutral. Without them his pride would have died out long ago.

He clenched his hands into fists when the sweet, almost sleepy female voice on the other end finally picked up. "Hello Niko, did you find her?"

"Yes and no. The demon popped her off campus, Morgan. Can you help me find her again?"

"Hmmm..." her voice reminded Caleb of those soothing instructions on yoga videos. "I can. Let me gather a few things and I'll text you her coordinates. Should've let me enchant your phone before you all left the pride in a huff."

Caleb rolled his eyes and turned to watch Xavier soothe the cop. He hadn't let them drive to Portland and he didn't regret it. He'd been able to see Piper, smell her – right before she'd thrown a damn book in his face.

He rubbed his jaw ruefully. It had stung a bit too. His surprise at the strength of the throw was what had allowed her to get away. Caleb had fucked up. He sighed and tried not to let the growl in his chest out.

When the witch had called saying she'd gotten word of their mate and that she was a human of all things had been a surprise, but that wasn't what had him booking his ass and the others to Sacramento. It was the news that the Florida Crocs had taken their blood feud to a whole new level.

Take the Alpha's mate and use her blood to curse the whole pride. And they'd gotten a demon to do their dirty work.

Caleb snarled and the cop glanced at him nervously.

"Chill dude, that's not helping the situation," Niko said, putting a hand on his shoulder. Instantly his touch soothed some of the irritation riding Caleb. "Morgan will find her. She's the most powerful witch in the Midnight Coven."

Niko was right, but it didn't help. With a damn demon he couldn't track her scent, popping from one location to the next like he had no sense.

"What did you think of her?" Caleb asked.

"Hard to tell when she's throwing books at your face," Niko chuckled.

A bark of laughter escaped him and Caleb rolled his shoulders back, easing more of the tension. "Yes, well. At least she's more capable than we gave her credit for."

"Seriously, a librarian? I never would have thought she'd bite that fucker like that," Niko admitted. "A hellcat if I've ever seen one."

Caleb tuned into the conversation Xavier was having with the dad. It would be best if they could get him to trust them.

Somehow his Second explained to the cop that they were just trying to help Piper, and that they were the only ones who could even find her.

The shell-shocked expression on the cop's face turned to suspicion, but he nodded when Xavier explained the security guard tried to snatch her from the library. He had a way with words that Caleb secretly envied.

Xavier clapped the cop on the back and then walked him over to Caleb and Niko. Xavier had a temper even Caleb was wary of, but he hid it behind his deep, soothing voice and a gentle expression. Nothing ruffled his fur...except Caleb.

So, this was Piper's father. Caleb could smell the familiarity. Her scent on another male who was not one of his partners raised his hackles even though he knew this man was no competition. That secretly wild, gorgeous woman was *his*.

And theirs.

"This is Richard, Piper's father," Xavier said, making the introductions.

"Sir, it's nice to meet you," Caleb said, stepping forward to shake the cop's hand.

The man glared at his hand but then shook it. "Xavier says you know what happened to my daughter and where to find her?"

Niko shook his hand next and nodded. "We do, sir. Well, we will in a moment."

"And how exactly do you know where she is?" Richard was suspicious and with good reason.

The three of them shared a look. How much should they tell him? Richard had seen something *disappear* with his daughter out of thin air. It would be impossible to explain that away. Xavier gave him a nod, agreeing to share their world with a human. After all...this was their mate's father. It would make things easier in the long run.

"Well..." Caleb drifted off, not sure where to start.

Caleb didn't know Piper – not really. But one whiff of her scent and his instincts had kicked in hard. Already he needed her in his arms. He needed to hear that whispery voice again – so husky and soft, like a cabaret singer's. Her strange green eyes reminded him of the ocean in the Caribbean, pure and untouched by man. How was her hair so black? It was darker than ink and the tanned skin surprised him, she didn't seem like the type to go outside much. Piper was a librarian after all.

For fuck's sake he knew nothing about this human woman and he had no idea how it was going to work between them.

Somehow they had to keep a human safe from a demon hell-bent on using her for some nefarious plan, and then convince her she wasn't just his mate. She was Xavier and Niko's as well. What would her father say about that?

"Morgan sent me the coordinates," Niko announced. "We should get going."

"Hey! No one is going anywhere until they explain to me what the hell is going on!" Richard shouted.

Caleb glanced at Niko. He could be the one to explain. Caleb couldn't fucking deal with a terrified human at the moment, not when his *mate* was out there with some demon. He strode off toward the truck and the others followed as he'd expected.

He ran his hand through his hair again and listened to Niko explain about the witches and the demons and the shifters this poor cop had no idea existed until two seconds ago. Caleb wished he could help the guy out, but he was barely holding onto his cool as it was.

The cop tagged along as Caleb led them back to the parking lot. Richard's rapid fire questions didn't surprise him. He seemed like a good cop – logical and more interested in facts than opinions and emotions. Niko answered everything from who they were to where they came from.

"Sir, look," Niko said, putting a hand on Caleb's arm so he would stop. "Let me give you my I.D. and Xavier and Caleb will too. You can run our info. I'll even give you my social security so you can run a background check."

Richard glared but he took the I.D.s Caleb and Xavier begrudgingly handed over. "You're telling me a witch told you that your mate – all three of yours, who happens to be my daughter, told you where she was. And that her blood is the key to a curse on your people?" he asked. "I just want to get the facts straight, if we can even call them that."

"Yes," Xavier said.

Richard glared up at Caleb when he handed him his social security card. Caleb didn't give a fuck, he had nothing to hide and he didn't want a cop on his ass the whole time he was trying to track down and protect his mate.

His mate.

After the last female leopard on the west coast was murdered he hadn't expected to ever have a mate. There were exceptions to every rule, but Caleb had never had that kind of luck. Not since the crocs had burned his house down with everyone but him inside it ten years ago.

And now they wanted Piper. Well, they had another thing coming if they fucking thought he'd let *that* happen.

"How am I supposed to believe you're some kind of shifter?" Richard asked, staring the three of them down.

For fuck's sake.

Caleb stripped and shifted into his leopard form, prowling around the cop while he scented the sudden fear on the air – not as strong as most though and that made him respect Richard.

"God dammit, Caleb," Niko muttered, pulling some witch

ball out of his pocket the size of a marble. He tossed it on the ground and purple smoke filled the area. "Change back. You have five seconds before the cameras are functional again. Morgan said it wipes up to twenty seconds total on the backend."

Caleb shifted again and yanked his jeans back up, glaring right back at Richard. "We don't have the time for this shit. Do you believe us now?"

Richard was pale but he nodded, hand slowly coming off his gun. "Fine, you're a leopard the size of a bear. Doesn't mean I want you being mates with my daughter."

"It's not really a choice," Niko explained. "It's a weird combination of magic, genetics, and fate."

His glare deepened and he grumbled something unintelligible. "Fine, she can decide when she hears about this. I'll follow you to the location, but I'm keeping these for now," Richard said, holding up their I.D.s and social security cards.

"We're the best chance your daughter has at staying safe," Xavier warned. "Without us she's going to end up a demon sacrifice."

Richard's massive eyebrows drew together as his frown deepened. He may not like what was going on, but he knew he was out of his element. "Let's get her back and then we'll talk."

"Whatever it takes to fucking go already," Caleb snapped. "The longer we take the less chance she's still alive when we get there."

Richard turned on his siren and his lights as he got into his vehicle and Caleb jumped into the truck that he'd illegally parked on the lawn. She better still be alive. He refused to lose another female he was supposed to protect.

CHAPTER THREE

PIPER

S uddenly there was air again and she could breathe. "What the *hell?*" Piper never cursed. Ever. Her dad had always been strict about it.

"I'm sorry about that," the security guard said with a wince. "I always forget about the air thing."

Piper turned around to glare at him, but was so surprised she blinked and froze in place instead. The security guard was no longer a security guard. His face was still just as inhumanly gorgeous as before, but he wore a grey suit that was impeccably tailored and probably cost more than her car instead of the uniform she'd seen him in.

"I'm Eisheth," he told her, eyeing her from head to toe.

It made Piper feel a bit self-conscious. She looked down at her comfortable flats and the flowy skirt that went down to her knees. Her belt accentuated her small waist and the button down shirt was crisp and white. She'd rolled up the sleeves to her elbows, but otherwise she wore what she normally wore. It was professional, comfortable, and practical.

"Well, what exactly did you just do to me?" she demanded, checking his arm for blood, but there was nothing. It was as though she'd never bitten him down to the bone from what she could tell.

The shock of their new location and too many strange things not adding up had her confused and not quite sure how to respond. She'd been ready to lose it and now she was just... numb. Was this even real? Suddenly she felt dizzy. Piper sat in the nearest chair and then realized she was in some kind of penthouse. She leaped up and looked around at the posh space.

"Please explain," Piper gritted out, turning back to Eisheth.

He grimaced and Piper crossed her arms over her chest.

"You have to understand. I was summoned. There's nothing I can do about it once I'm called. I'm under contractual obligation by the universe. If someone knows my full name they can summon me for a favor."

"Summon?" she asked faintly, dropping into the chair again.

Why was he talking like something out of Buffy?

"Yeah, can I get you something to drink?" he asked, tugging at his sleeves until they were just so.

"Something with alcohol," she said meekly.

Too many strange things. It was all starting to add up, but not in a way she could wrap her head around.

Eisheth poured her something with a smell that made her eyes water and handed it to her. Piper drank it down without question. She knew she needed it no matter how much it made her cough. "How can you be summoned?"

Eisheth studied her over the rim of his glass. "I'm a demon, sweetie."

"Right, of course."

"I'm pretty sure that bastard Forneus has been giving out my name like party favors. That's the last time I play poker with him." Eiseth glared at nothing in particular, but Piper couldn't look away from him.

He was charming and handsome in the way that most clean cut men were. His hair was a gentle brown with tons of little tiny curls. His skin was nice and tanned, but it was his sharp jaw and dark brown eyes that made him attractive. Even though he was physically beautiful with muscles even the suit couldn't hide, he made her nervous. Nope, not just nervous. This guy freaked her out.

He was a demon.

A flippin' demon.

Piper burst out laughing and set down her empty glass. There was just no way this was real. No possible way. She must have lost consciousness and that was why she didn't remember how they got to this place.

Standing up she checked for her phone, but found it nowhere. "I appreciate the drink, but I'm not into role playing games. It's late and I need to get home."

"I can't let you go, Piper Leigh Kostopoulos. I'm under contract to bring you to the crocs of Miami, Florida." He swirled his alcohol around in his cup and then poured more in.

Her breathing grew ragged when she heard him rattle off her entire name as though it was something precious – worth more than gold. And she supposed to a demon it might be. *No one* knew her middle name. No one. Her father had named her after her mother who had died from pre-eclampsia. There were two people in the whole world who knew about her mother, and she was one of them.

"How do you know my name?" she asked, letting him refill her glass. Piper kept her voice as calm as possible, but inside she was freaking out. This wasn't normal. It didn't happen to people in real life.

"A witch scried for you, Piper Leigh Kostopoulos." The demon's eyes narrowed as he studied her and she didn't doubt him. Her middle name wasn't on anything except her birth certificate. "Some stupid witch broke the rules. Don't worry though, she'll get what's coming to her."

"I would prefer if you called me Ms. Kostopoulos, or Piper," she told him with false bravado as she sipped at the drink this time. "So why did you bring me here?"

She needed to figure out what the heck was going on. Piper needed a better understanding of the situation. Maybe then she could...do – something? Years of studying ancient Egypt and the Macedonian Greeks hadn't prepared her for actual demons, but they did mention something like them a few times.

After all they believed in multiple gods and goddesses...

"Are you Eisheth the demon, a Jewish demon?" she asked, his name suddenly clicking into place.

He grinned wide and sat down on the couch next to her, resting an arm along the top of it like they were best friends. "Yes, though technically I'm an incubus and not a succubus. Altered history books are quite common. No one likes the gays is seems. Why, are you Jewish?"

Piper couldn't stop staring at him. She drank a good amount of the liquor; noting the way the demon's eyes seemed to change colors. "I'm not," she admitted. "We were Orthodox, but now I'm...agnostic I guess."

Why was it so easy to talk to him? She should be trying to run away, but honestly Piper was just tired. And she wanted to know everything this guy had to say. Maybe he was crazy, but maybe he wasn't.

"I brought you here, clever little human, because the crocs

didn't specify I had to bring you to them immediately. Only that I had two weeks to do it before the moon was at its apex or some shit like that." He waved his hand dismissively. "See, much like the fae, demons have to follow certain rules. If we're summoned, the summoner gets one demand. But if they aren't very, very careful how they word their contract then... well, the crocs had a witch's help. So they were better than most. I couldn't simply tear them to pieces when they broke the summoning circle."

Piper finished her drink and curled up against the back of the leather couch, facing Eisheth. This was literally insane. Fae were now somehow real? Well...he did teleport her. "Why not just kill me then? Wouldn't that make your life easier?"

Eisheth grinned at her and tossed back his drink. He set the glass down with a 'clink' and then tapped her nose. "Yes, but I like you and killing humans without cause is a no-no. Good way to get Jess on my ass which you do *not* want. Believe me."

Piper actually smiled at him. He was fun, easy to talk to, and wasn't hurting or restraining her. After their rough start she thought it was going rather well. She truly believed he hadn't wanted to come after her. "Who's Jess?"

"Jessica James, Demon Hunter," Eisheth said with a flourish. A snap of his fingers and a business card was in his hand. "Here, you're going to need this."

And then there was that little bit of trickery. This guy was a flippin' demon.

Piper took the card with a frown and then tucked it into her skirt pocket. "Why does a demon have a demon hunter's business card?"

"Look sweetie," Eisheth said with a sigh, tucking her hair behind her ear like a best friend would. "The paranormal world is complicated and has a lot of rules. I'm trying to help you out here. You seem like a cool chick, and I hate being summoned for bullshit like this."

He sighed again and straightened a cuff link. Piper didn't like the sound of this. At all. If she was feeling a little less scared and a little more sober she'd think she was imagining all of this, but Eisheth was clearly a demon. This was clearly... not normal.

"But you have two weeks until I will be forced to deliver you to the crocs," he told her. "Tell your kitty cats, call Jess... do whatever you have to, but get me out of this contract." Eisheth ran a long, elegant finger down her throat and it made her shiver. "Because this blood of yours is powerful. I don't want to know what someone could do with pharaoh's blood."

Then there were shouts and Eisheth looked up at the door with a smile. "Oh good, your mates are here. Don't be afraid, they're good guys deep down, but maybe don't let them kill me, yeah?"

Piper blinked and they 'popped' again. When she could breathe she was standing in front of Eisheth, but he wasn't touching her. "I have so many questions to ask you still," she whispered, taking a step back until she felt the demon against her back.

"Sweetie, with your mind you'd never be done asking me questions." Eisheth leaned down and whispered in her ear. "You really do look like her by the way."

Piper gasped when the door exploded in front of her and three angry men – no four including her father – burst into the penthouse. The three she didn't know looked like they could rip a body to pieces with their bare hands and her father had a gun pointed at the man—demon behind her.

"No!" she shouted, putting her hands up. "He's letting me

go." Wait, was he? Piper glanced over her shoulder and the demon gave her an encouraging nod and a thumb's up.

"Piper sweetheart, please explain," her father gritted out.

Eisheth popped out of the penthouse before anything else could happen. Definitely a demon. There was no other way to explain that disappearance and for whatever reason Piper liked that demon.

"Piper," her name on the strangers' lips sent a shiver down her spine.

Suddenly three large men she didn't know were in front of her, checking her for any harm. They charged the very air with their presence and intensity. She had to take a step back. "I'm all right, really," she promised. She gave the three men a nod of thanks and then went around them to hug her father.

It was past midnight and she was exhausted after the excitement. "I don't know what you know," she told her father. "But there's a lot to explain." Would he even believe her? Well, he did just see Eisheth disappear in thin air...twice.

Her dad nodded and kissed her forehead. "I got the gist of it. That's why I think these guys should stay with you. They're ex-military and can keep demons out of your house."

"Excuse me?" she asked, not able keep the disbelief from her voice. "I don't even know these men and you want them in my *house*?"

Her dad grimaced and adjusted the collar of his police uniform. "Sweetheart, I can't watch you twenty-four seven. If you want to be able to still go to work and live your life you'll let them stay nearby until we figure this out. Otherwise you're coming home with me and riding on my patrols. Maybe you'll even become my partner."

She crossed her arms over her chest. "You're really okay with this?" Piper glanced over her shoulder and none of the guys looked uncomfortable or even apologetic. The taller one with the green eyes and blond-brown hair crossed his arms over his chest too and frowned at her, but he didn't try to rush them.

Her dad heaved a huge sigh and glanced at the suspiciously silent men behind her. "They can turn into leopards. Caleb did it right in front of me. Apparently a witch sent them to help you because you're their mate."

Piper's mouth popped open in shock. She wouldn't believe it if it hadn't come from her father's own mouth. Her cop father who didn't believe anything he couldn't see, hear, or touch. "Yeah, the demon said something about mates," she whispered, turning to inspect the three men a little closer.

"I can't do anything about a teleporting demon. So far they all have clean records, medals of honor, and can protect you against demons in a privately owned place. I don't really like the idea of whatever this mate thing is, but I told them I'd let you decide what you wanted to do." Her dad glanced around the penthouse and then dismissed it "I trust you, Piper. I'll support whatever you want to do."

They shared a look and Piper knew her father didn't like it, but there wasn't much else they could do when they'd been thrown into the deep end. It was sink or swim now. Her dad shrugged and she knew they didn't have many options. Her father was the most practical, logical man she knew. If he thought this was the best choice it probably was.

"Okay, I'll let them stay in the guest room," she murmured.

Piper also wanted to know more about this 'mate' thing. What exactly did that entail? Why did they even want to protect her? She glanced over her shoulder as they left the penthouse and tried not to make it obvious she was scrutinizing them.

They were incredibly gorgeous and all three oozed a

sexual energy she could feel against her skin like phantom hands. Piper shivered and licked her lips. "I don't understand how I can have three...mates."

The green-eyed one gave her a feral sort of grin and then the other's brown eyes twinkled at her as though he were trying not to laugh.

Her dad sighed. "I don't want to talk about it. Let's go. I'll escort you all back to your apartment Piper."

The attitude Dad had about the boys made her smile a little. Whatever they told him on the way to the penthouse – whatever they'd shown him had been enough to convince him demons and witches and...shapeshifters? Were real.

Piper felt hyperaware of the guys. She could feel them behind her even though they didn't touch her. Knowing they were her mates made Piper feel a bit sheepish about her reaction in the library. They hadn't been trying to hurt her, but she also didn't think she really cared for the term 'mate.'

Whatever it was supposed to be, they didn't just automatically 'get her.' If they wanted Piper they were going to have to work for it.

Dad pointed at all three of them as they got into the elevator. "She calls me and she's not happy, I will shoot every one of you in the face."

"Don't worry sir, we'll make sure she's happy."

That voice rumbled over her and she shivered again.

Damn she was in trouble.

CHAPTER FOUR

NIKO

Piper's apartment wasn't far from the university. It was about twenty minutes with the way Caleb was driving – like he was terrified to hurt their human mate. Niko watched her out of the corner of his eye even though he faced the window and Xavier was in the front.

They'd figured she would feel more comfortable with him since he wasn't quite so intimidating. Sometimes being the beta had its moments. It hadn't always been easy though with his brothers. All of them thought they were tough alphas and liked to try and prove it.

Then one day they were sent off to deal with the crocs and never came back. Suddenly it was just him and his younger sister. Until she'd been murdered. Niko would never forget the look on his parents' faces when they got that knock on the door.

Niko glanced at Piper again and felt that strange pull. The one he never thought he'd get. The crocs had been picking them off one by one and targeting the females especially. But here was a female of his very own.

Piper glanced at him again and then looked away, adjusting her skirt. Niko couldn't help but watch her elegant fingers and he sniffed the air, breathing in her natural scent of lotus flowers. Laced among that was the sharp tang of her fear that was beginning to edge into something closer to anxiety which he could handle better. There was also that strange sulphur smell he assumed was from the demon.

No one had said a word since they'd all piled into Caleb's spacious truck, but they really needed to address a few issues. Her cop dad led the way and it was nice to have the escort... just in case. Humans were unpredictable, but they did listen to cops. They couldn't have had better luck.

But it did make the father more suspicious. He didn't want to trust them, but after what Caleb had shown him? It was kind of hard to deny the truth.

"What happened with the demon?" Niko asked, turning to face her and lounging against the door so he looked smaller. His arm went along the back of the bench and he waited patiently. He felt Caleb and Xavier's attention like a weight, but neither of them turned around.

"He gave me this," she said in that husky voice that promised to fulfill all kinds of sexual fantasies. Piper gave him a business card and their fingers brushed against each other. Her flinch confirmed she felt the electricity between them as well.

Niko cleared his throat as he inspected the card, trying to ignore how his dick twitched in his pants. "Jessica James?" he read aloud. "I've heard of her. But she's a demon hunter. Why would the demon give you this?"

Piper shrugged and licked her lips again. Niko cracked his

neck and tried not to stare at those full lips of hers. She was making this fucking difficult.

"He said he was contracted but didn't want to be," she explained. "Eisheth told me to call Jessica and find a way to break his contract in two weeks or he'd have to take me to Florida. Apparently there are specifics that were left out, like taking me to them right away and not offering me help."

Niko smiled. Clever demon. He'd studied up on them after Morgan had first called. They weren't inherently evil, but followed rules like the rest of the supernatural world. If they broke those rules Jessica took care of them.

But through the grapevine he'd heard she hunted all kinds, not only demons. She just liked how dramatic 'demon hunter' sounded. Gave the mortal humans who found her website a bit of relief.

Niko shook his head and punched in the number to call later. "What else did Eisheth tell you?"

"Eisheth?" Caleb cut in, his voice sharp. "*The* Eisheth?"

Piper nodded and then realized Caleb couldn't see her. "Yes, he said history hated the gays. Why, do you know him?"

Caleb let out another bark of laughter. The dude was so uptight it was unreal, but Niko would be too if he'd gone through what Caleb had. "No, I don't know him personally. But I do know of him. I'm Jewish after all."

Their mate cocked her head to the side to inspect Caleb and Niko felt a shiver go down his spine. There was this strange sense of recognition – like he knew her even though they'd never met before.

"Here," Niko said before he did something too forward. He needed to touch her, to take care of her somehow, but she was still so skittish. "You've still got some blood on your face." He pulled a handkerchief out of his back pocket and dabbed at her chin without physically touching her.

29

Piper's eyes widened as she watched him, but she didn't move away like Niko thought she might. Once he was done Niko pulled back, feeling a bit dizzy at her close proximity. Her scent was strong and heady. Piper watched him and then opened her mouth as though she were going to say something.

But Xavier interrupted. "Is this the place?" he asked.

Piper broke her gaze from Niko's and turned to look out the window.

Damn, this mate crap was no joke. Niko had no idea what he'd expected but it wasn't this. It wasn't the breathless feeling he felt in her presence or the magnetic attraction. Since the moment he caught her scent she'd become his Earth and he was the moon, forever orbiting her.

It had only gotten worse when he'd finally set his eyes on her.

"Yes this is the place. Are any of you allergic to cats?"

Niko burst out laughing. Her wide-eyed look of surprise only made him laugh harder.

Xavier glanced back at her with a smile. "No, we're not allergic. We uh, can turn into cats."

"Oh, right. I forgot about that."

Niko had to put his hand over his mouth. It shouldn't be so fucking funny, but after the stress of losing her and then finding her again, it was a much needed release. Though Niko could think of other ways to find a release. Too bad it would probably be a while.

"Niko," Caleb warned. "Get it together."

The dominant tone in Caleb's voice was the rock to the face he needed. Niko was just so damn nervous. Their pride had taken a beating the last few years. A mate was rare and precious and somehow...here she was.

"What kind of cats do you turn into again?" Piper asked. She placed the full weight of her gaze on Niko and he literally felt his heart stutter for a moment while he tried to think of a reply.

Caleb parked the car and the jolt brought him back to his senses a bit. "We turn into leopards."

Piper frowned and Xavier opened her car door for her. Then he held out a hand which she took without even thinking twice. Niko gritted his teeth and hopped out of the truck. Lucky bastard.

Caleb grabbed their bags from the back of the truck and tossed them at Niko. He caught them without looking and watched Xavier and Piper head to her father's cop car. She stuck her head in the window and Niko turned away so it wasn't obvious he was listening in.

Xavier gave them a bit of space, but it was clear he was listening to the whispers as well. They all were.

"Are you going to stay in the area?" she asked.

"Yeah, I'll tell them I need to be in this area while I'm on duty. I won't be far. I'll finish my shift, but I'll be here in a few hours like always." Then there was a pause. "You still have that gun I gave you?"

"Yes, of course Dad, but you know it's locked up. That's the law."

"Well unlock it and keep it close, just in case. I trust they're telling the truth and they're going to keep you safe, but they'll stay respectful or you shoot them, you hear?"

"Yes of course, Dad."

"I trust you, sweetie. You've learned everything I could teach you, and you have common sense. Use it, even if the situation is different." Niko could hear her dad sigh and then a kiss on his daughter's cheek. "Text me and keep me updated. Everything will be all right." Then he pulled off and Piper turned back around to face Xavier with a determined look on her face.

"Don't do anything to piss her off," Niko muttered, knowing the other two could hear him. "Think a book to the face sucks? Imagine a bullet."

This mate thing was way more complicated than he'd thought it would be. When they first got the news, Niko hadn't really considered all the extra shit having a human mate would entail – like distrust. Other shifters knew what to look for – they could feel it and smell it. But a human?

"As long as it's not in the face we'll heal," Caleb countered. "But be respectful and everyone keep their fucking hands to themselves unless she makes the first move."

Xavier gave them a nod and then followed Piper to her apartment after she waved good-bye to her father. The girl was so strange. Sure, she was gorgeous, but there was this odd aura she had about her. Niko could fall into her eyes and listen to her voice forever. He wondered what she would sound like if she sang.

"Take these bags upstairs and get whatever information from her you can. Then get her to relax and calm down. It's going to be a long two weeks if she can barely talk to us," Caleb ordered. He ran his hand violently through his light brown hair hard enough Niko was surprised there was still hair on his head at all. "I'm going to check the neighborhood and get a feel for the area."

Niko sighed and shouldered the bags. "You should talk to her. She's your mate too."

"We both know I make her uncomfortable." Caleb glared at him like it was *his* fault. Out of all of them their Alpha had it the roughest.

"At some point you're going to have to talk to her," Niko called after him. Caleb ignored him and disappeared down the street.

Niko followed that intoxicating scent of lotus blossom and

took a good look at the apartment building. It was nice, but generic in that way all apartment buildings were. The scent took him up to the second floor and down the hall to a corner apartment.

He could hear Xavier inside and tried the knob. It was unlocked and Niko looked around as he stepped in. The moment he crossed the threshold a black and white cat attacked his leg with a shriek.

"Christ on a cracker!" Niko tried not to kick the animal off him. It was not easy to juggle the bags and close the door so the cat couldn't get out. Damn those claws were sharp. "Can someone help me out?" he asked loudly, throwing a glare at Xavier.

The asshole was grinning at him with Piper giggling next to him. Yeah, well, he couldn't exactly blame him for not wanting to leave her side. Niko tossed the bags to the floor and snatched the back of the cat's neck like he would any one of the naughty kits in the pride.

The housecat snarled and hissed at him but Niko hissed back and let a rumble escape his throat. He was more dominant than a domestic animal for chrissakes. The cat arched back and tried to take a swipe at him anyways.

Niko sighed and inspected the markings on the cat before setting him down on the highest surface he could find. They were invading his territory after all. "Your white cat has black fur that looks like a vest," he noted.

Piper was smiling when he turned around and nodded. "Yes, that's why I named him Cat Solo."

"Cat Solo?" Xavier asked, going through every single cupboard in the kitchen.

Niko rolled his eyes and then winked at Piper. "Star Wars you dimwit."

"Never saw it."

33

Piper gasped as though the statement offended her personally. "I can't believe you've never seen it." Then she watched Xavier open the fridge. "Are you hungry?"

There was that cute little head tilt again. She was going to fucking kill him. Niko picked up the bag of weapons and tossed it on the table, wincing at the loud sound.

"Well we're all going to have to eat. Thought I'd cook something," Xavier told her. "But I don't see all the ingredients I need. When Caleb gets back I'll head to the store."

"So you all really plan to stay here for two weeks?" Piper squeaked.

Niko watched her face go pale and how she glanced between the two of them nervously. He nodded slowly. She really thought it wouldn't be a permanent situation. They had so much to explain in two weeks. Not to mention the issue of where the pride was located.

"You turn into cats and three of you are supposedly my mates, whatever that means exactly?" Piper tried to clarify.

She was starting to lose it.

Xavier barely noticed as he pulled out his phone to start typing out a list. "Technically we turn into leopards and until you're safe you can't be alone. We have to figure out a way to break the contract I guess." Wisely he didn't comment on the mate thing.

"And then you'll leave?" she pressed.

"If that's what you want." Niko put away the ball of witch doom Morgan had given him the recipe for and pulled out the sage instead. Piper was close to breaking and he had to make sure that didn't happen. "Why don't we get some air?" he asked.

She tore her eyes from Xavier and then looked at Niko. Her eyes flicked to the bundle of sage in his hand and Piper blinked as though she suddenly remembered she was the hostess. "Sure, I'll show you the balcony."

Niko shared a look with Xavier and tossed him the sage. "Demon proof the house. I'll...try to explain."

They knew when Morgan had told them their mate was a human that this wasn't going to be easy. And now a demon was in the mix? Niko only hoped that Piper was as practical as her father. No doubt a lifetime of weird, unexplained things he'd seen on the streets had made their stories credible along with Caleb's little trick right in fucking public.

After all Sacramento wasn't even their territory. They were only there with the permission of another freaking wolf pack. Niko couldn't wait to get back home and show Piper Crescent City. You know, if she didn't run off first.

CHAPTER FIVE

PIPER

At least it wasn't that hot. May could get so brutal sometimes. A cool night breeze ruffled Piper's disheveled hair. She didn't even care that she looked like a mess around three of the hottest guys she'd ever seen in her life. Like Niko – had she ever seen anyone with eyes as blue as his?

His blond hair was almost white and longer than Caleb's dirty blond, brownish hair. The two didn't look anything alike, but they were all leopards? How did that work exactly? Piper sighed and wrapped her arms around herself. It had been a very long day.

Niko closed the door behind them and she could hear him stop, probably to look around at the space she'd set up with the twinkling lights, but Piper didn't bother to look. His steps across the wood floor warned her. Niko stopped with very little space left between them, but he didn't touch her.

She could feel his body heat as he turned to lean his back against the railing. Niko propped his elbows up on the edge and eyed her like she may just explode and yell at him. Piper wanted to. It might make her feel better, but she was just so dang tired.

"Ask me anything," he told her. "I'll give you the truth even if it's not something you necessarily want to hear."

Piper narrowed her eyes. Was Niko appealing to the scholar in her? These...mates were more attuned to her than anyone else in her life had been excluding her father. "How would I know you're not just making stuff up?"

Niko made a cross over his heart and then held out his pinky finger. "I promise to tell you nothing but the truth."

"A pinky promise?" she asked. Her stupid mouth was turning up at the corner even though Piper was still annoyed. She shook her head and locked her pinky with his. It couldn't hurt.

"Pinky promise," Niko assured her. "Now what do you want to know?"

Goodness he was gorgeous. Piper could see the definition of his muscles with the way his T-shirt pulled as he leaned back on his elbows. He had this easy smile and looked at her like she was the only thing he gave a damn about. It was flattering and terrifying all at the same time.

"Well, can you prove to me you're a leopard?"

Niko chuckled. "Yes, but only inside the house. It's too populated here in the city. Someone could see me."

Piper chewed on her lower lip in annoyance.

Instantly Niko's gaze went to her mouth and she felt electrified. Piper couldn't stop watching him watch her. Did she really have that kind of power over him? She brought her hand up and rubbed her thumb across her swollen lip. Biting the shit out of a demon hadn't exactly been comfortable.

His eyes followed her thumb and Piper's skin tingled. The space between them was charged – electrified. It felt like lightning was about to strike and she wasn't sure what she thought about that yet. Why was he so...into her? They didn't even know each other.

"What exactly is a mate?" she finally asked.

Niko looked up and frowned. "What?"

His confusion almost made her laugh, but she bit her tongue. Piper didn't want him to think she was making fun of him. Out of the three guys Niko was the one she felt the most comfortable around.

"What is a mate?" she repeated.

The fog cleared from his eyes and he blushed a little. Piper couldn't believe this large, muscular man was blushing because of a simple question, or was it that she'd caught him staring at her lips?

"Well, it's kind of like a soul mate," Niko murmured, eyes dropping down to her mouth again before his gaze returned to her eyes. "But it's a little more than that – something to do with genetics and magic and fate. Cat shifters have more than one mate normally. The wolves only have one. There are a few other shifters and the rules are different for each of them like the foxes, but essentially a male is fated to one female within our pride. That you're human is probably because we have no females left except the baby."

Piper was rapt as he explained. It was a whole new world that had been living under the one she knew and she desperately wanted to know everything. Somehow these three men were fated to be hers? "So all three of you are my mates? You all don't mind, um...sharing?" she asked.

Niko gave her a lazy smile and shifted so he leaned on only one elbow and faced her, closing what little distance there was between them even more. Piper felt her heart beat faster, but she tucked a piece of hair behind her ear and ignored it. Just because magic and fate decided she was their mate didn't mean she had to do anything about it.

"Yes, you are our mate. The three of us are all yours. We don't mind sharing," Niko told her with that smile of his that made her stomach flutter. "It's the only thing we know. More males means more parents to watch the kittens, and the few females are well protected, though most of them don't need our help in that department. They're far more vicious and feral than we are." The way he looked at her – Piper knew he was thinking about the way she'd bit the demon.

She did feel a bit bad about that now that she knew Eisheth didn't want to deliver her at the end of the two weeks.

"What if I don't want to share? What if I'm not interested in any of you?" Piper asked, trying to sort out her thoughts and feelings. There was so much to take in and try to absorb. What were her options? There was a lot to process.

Niko stood up straight and she gasped as he towered over her. Piper had forgotten how tall he was and how intimidating he could be when he wanted. He stepped forward and she tried to step back but the railing hit her spine from the other side. She was trapped. Niko placed an arm on either side of her and stared down, that cocky smile growing wider – somehow still not touching her.

"Are you really not interested in us?" he asked, his voice husky and suggestive.

Piper felt it on her skin, rumbling seductively into her bones until she nearly vibrated with the sound of it, the feel of him so close, and his strange smell of night air on fur mixed with freshly cut grass. Her breath caught in her throat and Piper couldn't help the way she stared at his lips.

He was so close that if she turned, her mouth would brush against his. The warmth of his body warded off the cool night air.

"Um..." Was she interested? It was difficult to form a rational thought with his gorgeous body so close to hers. "I don't even know you," she finally whispered. "But I do feel physically attracted to you."

"Damn." Niko inhaled sharply. "You gotta stop doing that."

Piper blinked and looked up into his clear blue eyes. "Doing what?"

His smile widened into a grin and his gentle hand held her chin lightly. "Saying things that make me want to kiss you. Most humans aren't as honest as you are."

Her heart leapt into her throat and she couldn't help but glance at Niko's lips again. He really was beautiful. What would it be like to kiss him?

"Hey, Caleb is back so..." Xavier trailed off when he took in the scene but even his sudden presence didn't distract Niko. Piper glanced at Xavier and he had this amused expression on his face, like he thought they were the cutest thing ever. "So y'all gonna kiss or what?"

Piper felt her cheeks heat furiously and she ducked under Niko's arms to face Xavier, but he wasn't exactly safe territory either. The way he looked at her like he was hungry...she cleared her throat awkwardly. "What were you saying?"

Xavier grinned wide. "Caleb's back. I'm going to go grab a few things from the store. Want anything?"

"No thank you, Xavier. But I appreciate you asking."

Somehow Xavier didn't make any of it weird, and Piper appreciated that more than she could ever properly communicate.

She could feel Niko behind her – hyperaware of him in a way she'd never been with another human, but he wasn't human was he?

"Nah, thanks man. I'm going to make sure Piper doesn't have any other questions."

Xavier snorted. "Sure, you are. I'll be back in a bit."

Piper blushed again and sat at the picnic table in the center of her balcony. Since she had the corner unit hers was larger than the others. It was why she'd agreed to the higher price. Being outside could wash away a bad day like nothing else. It was one of her favorite places to study.

She picked up the lighter on the table and started lighting the various candles one by one. "So you want to make sure I don't have any other questions?" she asked without looking at Niko.

"Sure," he said, sliding onto the bench across from her. "It's why I'm here."

Piper eyed him, still feeling the heat from his proximity and the way she felt breathy and flustered just thinking about kissing him. She didn't want to talk about mates anymore. It led her down a dangerous path she didn't quite understand.

"You are all leopards, yet you look nothing alike. Also, leopards aren't even native to America. So how does that work?" Facts and science and history. Maybe with some of those she could find her place in this new world.

Niko flashed her a smile but it was sad as his expression grew serious. His eyes looked strange with the flame reflected in them and he tapped the wooden table with a finger as he thought. "Well, we're all American citizens, but like any normal human we immigrated. Xavier came from Africa and the pride there. Caleb is Jewish and I think his family emigrated from Israel at some point, making their way across Europe until they came here for the religious freedom. There are plenty of prides in the Middle East. And then my family came from Russia. We eventually created the pride here on the west coast, all of us from all over the world just like any other American."

Piper cocked her head and stared at Niko as she absorbed all that information. Instantly he stilled and reached across the table so fast she didn't even see him move. He grabbed her chin and leaned forward. Her heart stopped and for a split second she thought he was going to kiss her – and for the briefest moment she wanted it desperately. She wanted his hands in her hair, holding her close as he devoured her mouth, tasting the night and stars on him.

Goodness it had been a long time since she'd been kissed.

But then Niko pecked her cheek and stood. "You're adorable when you tilt your head like that," he told her as he stood. "Let me go get Caleb to answer the rest of your questions. I have to make sure Xavier didn't fuck up the demon proofing."

When he went back inside she could finally breathe again. Her lips tingled and he hadn't even kissed them. Piper brought shaking hands to her mouth and wondered how exactly she was going to handle three of the hottest men she'd ever met. They all wanted her and weren't afraid of showing it. Niko's restraint was impressive because she could practically *taste* his desire on the air.

There was also this tug on her heart, one that she knew would lead her right back to Niko if she turned around and looked. Some sort of bond was forming and Piper didn't know how she was going to handle it, let alone three of them.

The door slid open and Piper tensed. It was strange but she could *sense* this wasn't Niko. The energy felt different and the sheer insanity of that scared her. They'd spent all of twenty minutes with each other. What would it feel like after two weeks?

Caleb didn't say anything as he walked around the picnic table, inspecting every nook and cranny before looking at her.

"There aren't any spiders out here," she told him.

He frowned at that. "What do you mean?"

Piper waved her hand at the various plants she had. "The mint, citronella, and lemongrass keep the spiders away. In case you were concerned."

Caleb stared at her in disbelief. One corner of his mouth even twitched like he wanted to laugh or smile. "I'm not afraid of spiders."

Piper smirked and looked down at her hands with a shrug. The scary one had a sense of humor somewhere deep under that prickly exterior of his. Maybe he was more like her father than she wanted to admit.

"Niko told you about mates but let me explain the crocs to you," Caleb said, taking control of the conversation. He leaned against the balcony with his arms crossed over his chest. She found it interesting he wouldn't get any closer to her – like *she* made *him* nervous. Caleb couldn't be more different than Niko if he tried.

"Okay," she murmured, letting her fingers trail over the flames of her candles. Caleb had a gruff voice she actually liked. It was...gravelly yet tender, like he could never direct his irritation at her.

Caleb watched her for a moment, but said nothing about the fire. "Cat shifters don't have many enemies or predators. Our biggest danger is each other, but we haven't starved for many centuries so we leave each other alone for the most part. We have had to compete with others for territory rights and there are some we just don't like much. The wolves have always been difficult to get along with, but that's just part of our animal natures. As humans we understand each other and follow the laws and rules of our world. There hasn't been a war over territory – at least on the West Coast – for over a century."

The historian in her fell under Caleb's spell. He was speaking her language and she was starved for more information. Piper couldn't help the way she stared at him without blinking, lips slightly parted as her imagination ran wild with the possibilities of his words.

Wolves and leopards banding together to form peace. Witches helping them keep this peace. And then the possibility of other shifters. They'd already mentioned foxes and crocodiles. What else was out there? What else could she learn with these three?

"When cat shifters first came to America, most of us preferred the warmer climes so we went south, but there was already a shifter who'd claimed the south and didn't want to share," Caleb went on, his gaze as unblinking as hers. They stared at each other as if they were both in some sort of trance. "Both sides claimed the other started the blood feud. But all I know is that our pride moved west and the crocs wouldn't let it go. They came after us regardless of how much space we put between us and them."

Piper blinked when she realized he was done, but she knew there had to be endless details he was leaving out. "Are there books on these events?" she asked.

Caleb frowned and uncrossed his arms. He ran his hand through his hair and sighed, looking away from her for the first time since he started talking. This one out of all three of them was the only one who wanted to hide himself away from her.

For whatever reason that made Piper want to know even more about him.

"I suppose there probably are," Caleb admitted. "But the

witches are the ones who take care of all the lore. You'd have to ask them."

Piper stood from her spot and crossed the balcony to stand by his side. Caleb wore nothing but a black tank top and black jeans. His boots were scuffed leather, but they looked good on him. If he was also supposed to be her mate then why didn't he seem to like her?

His large arms made her want to touch him. Even though Caleb scared her a little, he was the most mysterious of the three. "What else?" she asked, looking up into those unreadable green eyes.

They glittered darkly at her, and his frown deepened, but Caleb obliged her. "My pride has been at war with the crocs for generations. The killing never stops. When I was fifteen they set my house on fire with my brothers and sisters and parents inside. Burned them alive while they slept. All ten of them. I was lucky to be out on one of the battlefields hunting croc, but I came back to nothing but smoldering ashes."

Piper felt her heart clench and tears prick her eyes. It physically hurt, right in her chest. The pain in his voice was thick even though he tried to hide it. Somehow she felt his pain and she had to do something. So she took his hand in her two small ones. It was all she could offer him, and Caleb's eyes widened.

"My father was the pride Alpha and so I took his place. I've been leading them ever since. But I'm not the only one who's lost family. Niko, Xavier...the Klamath Mountain Pride only has fifteen members now. No females left except one and she's barely a year old – an orphan we managed to save from Tahoe."

"Is that why they're after me?" she asked. No females meant genocide in a way. And no more pride meant no more competition for the crocs.

"Yes. With you the pride has hope. There could be other humans out there for the other males. The witches are doing the best they can, but the crocs have a dark witch on their side. There aren't many hunters out there and without an official kill order from the Council...I'm just trying to keep my pride alive as long as I can."

Piper took a deep breath and then stepped forward, wrapping her arms around Caleb. She hugged him because he needed it. There was so much tension and stress and pain and fear in him. She could feel it and now...now he had to worry about her and some demon. It hardly seemed fair.

"Let me help. I'm sure if I had access to some real paranormal books I could find a way to break the demon's contract. After all, research and studying are what I'm good at." Piper stepped back and looked up into Caleb's green eyes.

His expression was unreadable but he nodded. "I'll have Niko call Morgan. She'd know better than us."

Piper blushed and looked back inside at Niko going through that large black duffel bag of his. He wasn't looking at her, but rather staring at Cat Solo on the cat tree while her cat flicked his tail. After their almost kiss she felt weirdly guilty for hugging Caleb.

This was all so confusing.

"Thank you," she said, turning back to him. He was so dang tall and just...delicious looking. It was difficult not to touch him again. And she wanted to, badly. "For trying to save me earlier tonight. And um, I'm sorry about throwing that book at your face."

For the first time she saw Caleb smile and Piper gasped. There was a strange sensation in her belly and she felt warm all over. The smile turned him into a god – that was how attractive and beautiful Caleb was.

"I like that you can take care of yourself," Caleb told her. He tugged on a piece of her hair, but otherwise didn't touch her. "And you're very creative about it. I'm waiting to see what you'll do next."

Piper cleared her throat and tried to remind herself she never reacted to boys—men like this. For a long time she'd dated, but it was so awful and demanding on her time she gave it up. She had decided living alone with a million cats was the way to go.

Well now she had three more cats. Though they weren't exactly what she'd pictured.

But, maybe they were better?

"Let's go see what Morgan has to say," Caleb said, pushing off the balcony and striding toward the apartment. He certainly knew what he wanted and didn't wait around to take it.

It made Piper wonder, was she something he wanted?

And why did she care so much?

CHAPTER SIX

PIPER

Piper sat up in bed and clutched the blanket to her chest. For a moment she wondered if she'd dreamt it all, but then she heard a distinctly male snore from the guest room. No, there were three men staying with her until they could get the demon situation handled.

The demon.

It still felt strange to think it was all real and not some horrible joke. Although the three guys currently passed out all over her apartment also happened to be able to shift into leopards, so you know...par for the course she supposed.

Piper pulled her phone off the charger and checked the time. It was still a bit early for her and after the surprisingly delicious meal Xavier had cooked she'd gone straight to bed. She had no idea when the others went to sleep but it had been nearly three in the morning when she'd closed her eyes.

Thankfully they'd mostly left her alone. Piper enjoyed the quiet conversation at dinner, but they seemed to be able to tell she was overwhelmed and exhausted.

Only ten in the morning and she had three messages from her father. Piper tapped his contact and waited. He picked up on the second ring. "Hey sweetheart, everything still okay?"

"Yes, these strangers didn't kill me," she joked.

He grumbled something indiscernible and then said, "I came by earlier, but you were already asleep so I went home to nap and shower. While I was on duty I ran their licenses and did a background check. All of them are clean and employed. They don't have medical records or I'd have those too."

"Thanks Dad, I'm glad they're good guys." Piper didn't think they'd hurt her. If they'd really wanted to they would have already. "I have to go in to the library for a few hours today."

"What time? I thought you had Saturdays off."

She picked at the thread coming out of her comforter. There was a lot more at the library than just work. "I'm going in after lunch. I switched with one of the other librarians. If I need to take a few days off I can."

"Good. I picked up our usual. I'll be by in twenty."

Piper didn't bother to say goodbye. Her dad hung up and she tossed the phone on the bed.

Thanks to Niko's contacts with the witches, Morgan had been very helpful. She'd gotten in touch with Sacramento's coven and set up a contact for Piper. The witch fully supported her desire to read everything she could on the situation. It could only help after all.

Piper had learned from Morgan that there was a whole other secret library underneath her own at Sacramento State. They hid in plain sight apparently. The university had entire paranormal classes that didn't exist to the public – you had to know someone to get access to them.

Honestly, at this point nothing surprised her.

She slipped out of bed and tried to make as little noise as possible while she showered. Piper was excited to see what was in this secret library that only existed for the paranormal world. The witches were the keepers of lore. What Piper wouldn't give to see some of their older texts.

What languages would they even be in? Piper had learned Ancient Egyptian, some Ancient Greek and Latin, and a bit of Sanskrit. It was enough to get her by when it came to her studies and research. Although she wished she was more fluent in Sanskrit and Greek. It was just so long ago and they were all dead languages.

Most scholars were guessing at this point.

The most reliable texts were in the original forms so she usually stuck to Latin and Egyptian for the most part. Even took a bit of modern Arabic to see if that would help. All that studying and she'd only been to Cairo the one time. Piper sighed and brushed her wet hair out. One day she would go back to find out what really happened to the Library of Alexandria.

As she came out of the bathroom Piper ran right into someone hard enough she almost lost her hold on the towel.

Xavier stepped back and tried not to smile. "I'm sorry, I was just going to knock and let you know your dad is here."

Piper couldn't stop staring at him. The broad shoulders and large chest filled her vision and finally she looked up into his eyes that seemed more golden than brown today. Xavier's dark skin was flawless and it reminded her of some of the depictions of the Egyptian gods.

Out of all three of the guys, Caleb was the most reserved and Niko the sweetest, but Xavier was a bit of a mystery. He was sweet and gentle with her but there was always this edge he stood on. Like it would take nothing to shove him over the precipice and unleash chaos and destruction.

"Thank you," she said, feeling a little breathless and tightening her grip on the towel just in case it fell at an inopportune time. "Please tell him I'll be right out after I get dressed."

Xavier gave her a slow, lazy smile and her heart pounded in her chest. Piper had a hard time getting a read on this one even if she could see how he seemed to take care of the others. But...she wouldn't put it past him to simply tug the towel out of her hands and press her against the wall.

Piper licked her lips as she tried to tell herself that wasn't what she wanted – that she'd rather he just go in the other room and wait for her, but that fire in her belly shot straight down to between her legs and lord almighty it had been *way* too long since the last time she'd gotten any.

"It would be my pleasure," Xavier murmured. He didn't move forward, but it felt like he was surrounding her anyways.

"Your pleasure?" she asked. Piper didn't like the way her words were practically a gasp. The man hadn't even touched her and already she was breathing hard and losing her damn mind. "To do what?"

He raised one eyebrow at her and that smile widened. It just wasn't fair how gorgeous he was. "To tell your father you'll be out soon."

"Oh right." Had she really gotten so distracted she'd forgotten what they were talking about? "Can you leave now?" Goodness gracious she was worse than a teenage boy.

Xavier grinned and left, quietly closing the door behind him. Once he was officially gone she crossed the room and locked the door. Then she finally took a deep breath and slumped onto the foot of her bed.

Was this part of what being a mate was all about? This undeniable attraction and almost...ravenous desire and hunger? It made feelings Piper didn't know she had stir in her chest. Xavier cooking the night before had somehow been the most sensual thing she'd ever seen. The way he made sure she liked everything had her heart melting...but still she didn't really know him, or the other two.

Well, except Caleb. Surprisingly she knew more about him than she did even Niko though their connection was a lot thinner. It didn't even seem like Caleb liked her very much. She was more of a nuisance. He hadn't *chosen* her to be his mate.

Piper threw on a bra and a white T-shirt that was made of the softest material. It was one of her favorite shirts and Saturday was far more casual at the library. So she grabbed her favorite blue-jeans that she thought personally made her ass look amazing. But she was not wearing it for them. She wasn't.

The trinkets across the top of her dresser made her pause. It was a bunch of random items she'd picked up here and there but her eyes caught on the scarab beetle necklace she'd bought on her last trip to Egypt.

The woman had sworn it was inscribed with sacred spells to protect against evil and possession. Piper had worn it into the tombs just to be safe. She traced the lapis lazuli of the wings and slipped the gold around her neck. It couldn't hurt to wear when there was a demon contracted to deliver her to crocodiles.

Then just for good measure, Piper put on the gold Uraeus bracelet with the rearing cobra. The items hadn't been cheap, but apparently she had the blood of pharaohs. At the time it had seemed like a good idea and she was glad for them now. They may just be more than jewelry after all with what she'd recently learned.

She opened her door a crack and heard her father's gruff

voice and Xavier's smooth, velvety one. What were they even talking about? Piper peered through the crack and saw her dad in his usual place on the recliner with Cat Solo in his lap purring like mad. The coffee and kolaches and donuts were on her dining room table.

Xavier was explaining to her dad that his family made something similar but the spices in their kolaches were different. Surprisingly her father was interested and admitted he'd like to try something like that some time.

Who was this man and what had he done with her real dad? Richard Kostopoulos had not liked one single boyfriend of hers. Always said they weren't good enough for her. But somehow he liked all three of these guys?

There had to be some magic talisman they'd brought to appease irritatingly overprotective Greek fathers.

"Piper you want some of this?" Xavier called. He winked at her from the table as he set the food out for everyone. He grabbed plates and silverware, even putting out water and cream and sugar.

She blushed and opened the door all the way. Somehow Xavier had known she'd been listening. Damn cat ears probably. "Yes please," she said quietly, stopping to peek in the guest bedroom.

Niko and Caleb shared the queen-sized bed easily, one on each side with enough space between them for someone else to fit. Piper cleared her throat and ignored the thought of her in between, snuggled by both.

What the heck was wrong with her? Piper had never been one to consider multiple boyfriends before, but the way these three were together...that tug she felt in her chest that drew her to them was undeniable.

She shrugged and went to kiss her father on the cheek in greeting. He tapped her necklace with a smile but didn't say anything. Egypt had been her first trip alone and it had been hard on the both of them, but also good. It had strengthened his trust in her and soon after she'd been allowed to get her own place. It had also given her the courage to move out of the house in the first place.

Piper grabbed a kolache with ham and cheese and fixed her coffee while Xavier watched. He made his own plate and then sat on the couch all without ever looking away from her. His skill was impressive and the attention flustered her.

She spilled some hot coffee on her hand while those amber eyes entranced her. "Son of a biscuit," she muttered, shaking her hand out to dissipate the pain. Just her luck the Greek café made their coffee at a thousand degrees.

Instantly Xavier was at her side and examining the burn. His touch was gentle but he gritted his teeth hard enough she worried he'd crack them. "Here, let's get this under some cold water and I'll find the burn cream."

"Really, I'll be fine," she protested. But Xavier wasn't really a man one argued with. The way he moved and spoke – she barely realized she'd already obeyed when she was standing at the sink with her hand under the cold water.

Xavier rummaged in one of the duffels and her father sipped his coffee while he watched them. "You should put onions on it, my mother always put onions on everything," he told her.

"Dad," Piper sighed and tried not to roll her eyes. "That's not a real thing. Grandma was just extremely...superstitious." Her great-grandmother had come straight from Greece and her grandmother had grown up with all the same culture and superstition.

"I saw these boys laid out salt. There must be some truth to these superstitions," he told her; sipping that scalding coffee like it was nothing.

Piper turned off the water and dried her hand. "Yes, Dad. What's the salt for?" she asked Xavier when he took her hand to gently rub the burn cream in.

"Keeps out all kinds of things," Xavier muttered, eyeing the burn. "Doesn't look too bad, but you should take some Tylenol."

It was difficult not to smile. "I'll be fine, I'm a big girl. But do you have a sticker or a lollipop for being good?"

The question snapped him out of whatever funk he was in and Xavier blinked. Then he looked up and examined her face, searching her eyes for – something. Then there was that slow, lazy smile that made her toes curl and heat flood her. "I don't have a lollipop, but I could improvise."

Her mouth popped open in shock at the blatantly sexual innuendo. Then Piper realized what that might look like and immediately snapped her mouth closed. She couldn't help but laugh even though she felt her cheeks burning. "I'll think about it," she teased.

Piper grabbed her coffee and plate before taking her spot on the couch, leaving Xavier to figure out what she meant by that. As much as they intimidated her, Piper loved how easy it was to get under their skin.

She turned the TV on and took a massive bite out of her kolache. Maybe it wouldn't be so bad to have them stay with her for a bit. After all, having a bit of fun wasn't the same thing as agreeing to be their mate for the rest of her life.

CHAPTER SEVEN

XAVIER

Xavier threw a kolache at Caleb and then Niko hard enough both cursed him up one side and down the other as they rolled out of bed. "Piper's dad is here and she has to be at the library in an hour. Get up."

He would be the first to admit he was still on edge. Watching Piper disappear with the demon...just 'poof' – nothing left but air and the lingering scent of lotus blossoms had been almost as bad as watching the crocs rip his mother out of their home. As a seven-year-old boy he hadn't been able to do anything – but he'd tried and nearly gotten ripped in half for the trouble.

Two of his dads hadn't been home during that incident. They'd been dealing with the crocs they thought were on the border. The crocs hadn't been there though. Someone had given their pride bad intel and an entire group of them had snuck into their territory, killed his third father and took his mother.

His two dads came back and they hadn't really ever been

the same since. They were shells of the men they used to be. Xavier had been on his own for the most part, taking care of them when he could.

And this fucking demon just snatching Piper like that had brought all those memories roaring back. His scars hurt and itched more than they had in years. It hadn't been easy pretending everything was fine, but the scent of her fear had him bottling up any negative emotions. She was nervous around them still though she hid it well. Xavier didn't want that fear to turn to terror when he lost his temper.

But...that sly little joke Piper had thrown his way had settled him immediately. If her father hadn't been sitting in the same room Xavier would have kissed her for it.

And the girl was sexy as fuck. Just seeing her almost kiss Niko the night before...Xavier wanted to be the first to kiss her. After all Caleb was the one who'd spotted her in the library first. Caleb was the first one she'd laid eyes on so Xavier would be the first one she tasted.

He eased his expression back into something neutral for Piper and flopped down on the couch next to her, watching her without directly looking at her. She and her dad were watching some cyberpunk-looking show on Netflix. Xavier figured he had some catching up to do if she was a Star Wars fan. Maybe he could talk her into watching all of them with him as a date in her preferred order.

Xavier may live in the middle of nowhere but he didn't live under a rock. He knew the order of viewing was a controversial point.

"So who's going to be inside the library with me?" Piper asked, never once taking her eyes from the TV.

"I am," Xavier replied at the same time Caleb said it. His Alpha glared as he crossed the living room but didn't argue.

Niko blinked sleepily and held up his hands. He went

straight for the coffee, staying out of the argument as usual. "I'll be wherever I'm needed," he said.

Xavier tried not to growl. He couldn't help his annoyed frown. They'd barely made progress with Piper, but he supposed the demon's contract came first. It was difficult to ignore his mate with her scent surrounding him, inside him as he breathed in the air of her apartment.

All he wanted to do was show her what it could be like with them, how they'd care for her, and make her happy, but they had to deal with this fucking demon contract. Xavier gripped his mug of coffee hard enough it creaked. He set it on the side table before it shattered.

All he wanted was to snuggle with Piper on the couch and give her a foot massage while they watched Star Wars. But Xavier was still terrified he'd mess this up. His fathers hadn't been able to keep his mother safe and neither had he. How in hell was he going to keep Piper alive and out of the crocs' hands?

He glanced sideways at her and studied that strong, stubborn jaw of hers with the delicately tanned skin. Like being in the sun was an afterthought and the light had marked her with a tender touch – knowing how gentle she was.

Piper was the strangest woman he'd ever met. She was quiet, soft-spoken when she did talk, and she never once cussed. But then she liked Star Wars and Ancient Egypt and made little quips that had him stopping short. Xavier had heard from Niko that she'd implied Caleb was afraid of spiders. Xavier had to go outside and 'check the perimeter' so he could laugh his ass off without his Alpha hearing.

Glancing at Piper again he rested his hand on her calf and slouched a bit more on the couch. She tensed under his touch but didn't move away. Eventually as the show went on she even relaxed while Niko sat on Xavier's other side, tucked in close.

It had never been strange to be so physically close with Niko. The two of them had always been best friends and tactile comfort was common in the pride unlike the human males who were starved for it.

Then he felt Piper's attention like a hot brand. She snuck looks at him and Niko who leaned against him while he ate. Xavier smiled and put his arm around Niko's shoulders. The other male didn't even react. It was normal for them, yet Piper squirmed underneath his hand like she enjoyed what she saw.

Caleb settled at the dining room table, always a little apart from them. Sure, he was the pride's official Alpha but the guy needed to relax. He was always so serious and the whole mate thing had really thrown him for a loop. Xavier would feel more sympathetic if Caleb wasn't such a grating ass most of the time.

Maybe Piper would help him calm the fuck down.

Slowly Xavier started massaging her calf, keeping his eyes on the TV. He should probably keep his hands to himself with her father in the same room, but Richard had taken the whole 'there's a secret paranormal world' thing surprisingly well.

After he'd calmed him down and Caleb had shifted he'd taken it all in stride. The man was a cop for fuck's sake. There was plenty he'd seen on the streets without realizing it. Most cops took it better than the other normals.

The show ended and the only one who moved was Richard. He turned off the TV and went to see what Caleb was doing. The shiny guns and various different weapons had caught the cop's attention of course.

"Don't worry, sir. I have permits for everything," Caleb said, always the Boy Scout.

Xavier on the other hand didn't always like following the

rules. His hand traveled up Piper's calf toward her thigh and with his supernatural hearing he could pick up her tiny gasp and the acceleration of her heart beat.

Niko glanced over at the two of them, picking up on the sounds as well. His grin matched Xavier's own and Niko casually placed his arm over Xavier's lap to hide his hard on. Piper's lips parted when she noticed it as well, and then realized Niko was touching it.

She jumped off the couch like she'd been burned and her cheeks were red. "I need to finish getting ready." Piper disappeared back into her room and Caleb glared at the both of them.

Xavier shrugged, not giving a fuck what Caleb thought.

"Damn, you smell that?" he asked Niko, keeping his voice low enough Richard couldn't hear it.

Niko got up with a lazy stretch. "She definitely wants us," he murmured. "The scent of her arousal is enough to drive me mad."

It was difficult to get comfortable with how hard his dick was. Xavier went into the guest room to grab his boots and jacket. Piper was definitely interested. Maybe they'd be able to make their claim by the time the demon business was sorted out.

Niko grabbed his own shit and started getting dressed. "You need me to take care of that?" he asked, nodding at the giant bulge in Xavier's pants.

It was a tempting offer, but now that they had a mate... "I'd rather wait for her," he admitted. "We never thought we'd get a mate after everything, but we knew the two of us would be paired together if we did find her." Xavier adjusted his dick and sat down to pull on his boots. "I think I should wait until we can have her together, and talk to her about it. Piper isn't a shifter. Her culture is completely different from ours, but I'd still rather have her permission first."

Niko nodded. "Sounds like a plan. It'll be interesting to have Caleb as our third. I had no idea we'd end up with him."

Xavier snorted, annoyed all over again. "Me neither." Sometimes he thought he should have ended up Alpha of the pride, but Caleb had taken over young and managed to keep what was left of them alive for the most part. He respected that.

Caleb was the one who'd saved the orphan leopard in Tahoe. That little girl had the entire pride falling all over themselves to take care of her. Xavier knew Caleb was the best Alpha for the pride, but that didn't mean he had to like him. The guy needed a good hard fuck so he could relax and stop riding Niko and Xavier like they were green soldiers who knew nothing about their jobs.

"We should go before we make Piper late," Xavier muttered, hoping the witches had some answers in their library. If they didn't they'd have to deal with Jessica James, and he'd rather not if at all possible. That girl was crazy.

"There are only a few people here on Saturdays," Piper explained.

Xavier was on one side of her and Niko the other while Caleb brought up the rear and watched their backs. Richard had followed them to the university and then headed to the police station to start his shift. The man kept almost the same hours Piper did.

It was smart and Xavier was impressed at Richard's dedication to his daughter. He didn't know what had happened to Piper's mother, but he assumed that was why

Richard was so close to his daughter. It reminded him of his own broken family and how he wished just one of his dads had reacted like that. It would have made his life a thousand times easier.

But that wasn't life in the Klamath Mountain Pride. Xavier knew that. Nothing was ever easy.

"If you need me you can text me," Piper told Niko. "But most of the students don't need anything on Saturdays."

Piper was in her element. The way she walked with her shoulders back and her spine straight...Xavier licked his lips. She looked fine as hell in those obscenely tight jeans too – like she knew exactly what she was doing wearing them.

And that ass...fuck she was tempting him.

"I'll check the campus," Caleb said. "We can't ward off the demon here on public property, but I'll do what I can."

Piper threw a dazzling smile at Caleb over her shoulder and the Alpha blinked, completely dazed by her beauty and the infectious energy she radiated. Well, maybe there was hope for their Alpha after all. It was the first time Xavier had ever seen Caleb affected by anyone after what had happened to his family.

Something about being back at the university had Piper looking and sounding more confident. Out of all of them she wasn't worried about the demon, since apparently they were best buds now. No, she was practically skipping through the building because she wanted to see books.

It was fucking adorable and Xavier wanted to give her every book in the world if that's what would make her smile like that all the fucking time.

Piper threw open the doors to the library and searched for their witch contact – someone named Oscar that Morgan had arranged for them. Xavier had to pick up his pace to keep up with her, that's how excited she was. It was the first time since he'd spotted her through the library stacks the day before that he felt his heart lurch and stutter.

She was breathtaking.

Xavier felt himself falling for her. He was desperate to know her mind as well as her desires. Piper captivated him then and there and that rope that connected them tied around his heart and the bond strengthened. There was no going back for him now. She was it.

"Piper Kostopoulos?" someone asked.

Instantly Xavier was on alert and moved closer to her.

Piper's face lit up. "Oscar?"

God, what he would give for her to look at him like that. One glance at Niko, and Xavier knew he wasn't the only one to feel that way.

"I was told by Morgan to allow you into the library," Oscar stated. The witch didn't seem happy about the command.

Who the hell was this Morgan that a coven in another state and city did what she asked? Xavier shook his head. He stayed the hell out of witch business. That was Niko's specialty.

"I'll stay up here," Niko promised, brushing his hand against Piper's. Then his best friend caught his eyes over the top of her head. "Keep an eye on her at all times."

He nodded. Xavier refused to let her out of his sight. He'd never trusted witches and didn't plan to now. They had way too much power for him to ever feel truly comfortable around them. The witch who'd said Niko and Xavier would be mated to the same female all those years ago had been enough to keep him away for most of his life.

Until her.

Caleb gave them a nod and went back outside. Oscar inclined his head and led them through the library. Xavier placed his hand on Niko's shoulder as they passed. "Stay safe," he muttered. Niko was one of the nicest guys in the pride, but that didn't mean he was soft. After his sister, there was a dangerous edge to the male.

Whoever tried to come at them wouldn't leave in one piece.

Oscar took them through the massive library to the library's gallery where various sculptures and art were displayed. Then he led them to the darkest corner of that gallery. The witch sketched a design on the wall and when the last rune was inscribed the pentagram flared to life right before the edges of the door appeared. Oscar opened it and stepped aside.

Piper was in complete awe. She stared at the door and then took a tentative step forward. Xavier wanted to go first, but witches were neutral. It was more likely an attack would come at his back. He waved the witch in next, glancing over his shoulder, and then followed them both inside.

The door disappeared into a wall behind them and witchlight lit up the hall. Oscar led them down, and it was definitely down, for a good few minutes. The hall turned into a spiral and suddenly at the bottom it opened up into a massive space. The walls were stone and felt ancient. Xavier didn't want to look too closely at the runes and carvings on the pillars.

Tables were scattered about and stacks and stacks of books covered the three stories. The witch library went on forever and Piper looked like she might cry. The space felt loved and lived in which relieved him.

It was hard to tell sometimes how witches felt about anything.

"Morgan told me to gather some books regarding demons which are over there on that table. It's in the back near the section on demonology. You're a librarian and a scholar from what I know of the university staff. I'm sure you'll be able to figure it out. Need anything else and I'll be over there," Oscar said, pointing to an office off the main space.

Piper wasn't even listening. She was already walking toward the table Oscar had pointed out and she walked fast when she wanted to. Xavier cursed and jogged to catch up. The power in the library was palpable and he could taste it, like chewing on aluminum.

His mate's fingers trailed the wooden shelves and Xavier wished she'd touch him like that. The thought was all it took for his dick to harden again. Christ it was going to be difficult to concentrate around this woman.

No one in his generation had found their mate yet, so this was all new territory. Xavier didn't know what new mates were like and had no idea what to expect. But if this was it, fuck. They were in trouble, because all he could think about was grabbing that ass of hers and bending her over one of these tables so he could take her – mark her with his scent.

"Wow, this place is amazing," she whispered – most likely feeling the weight of the place as well. "There are so many books."

Xavier stopped and checked the books waiting on the table. He ran his hands over all of them to be sure, and then handed her one. Piper frowned and sat down with a shrug. "Some witch books aren't friendly," he explained. "And others are cursed. I wanted to make sure there was no funny business before you touched one."

Her look of surprise turned into a smile. "That was sweet of you," she murmured in that husky voice that only made his dick harder. "You're so nice to me."

Xavier sat down beside her, feeling flustered and pleased all at the same time. That she even noticed made him giddy.

"Well, you are my mate and you deserve to have someone care about you." He cracked open a book to hide the way he watched her. At least it was in English and wouldn't make him look like an absolute idiot.

"What's it like to have one mother and three fathers?" she asked, opening her own. "This is normal right, part of your culture?"

God, her question was so innocent, but it hurt like hell. "I don't remember," he told her honestly. "The crocs killed one of my fathers and took my mother when I was only a kid. Nearly tore me in two when I tried to get her back. I don't know what happened to her after that."

Piper stopped what she was doing and turned to face him fully, even moving one leg over the bench so she straddled it. It distracted him from the pain and the memories and he turned to face her the same way so that their knees touched.

"I had no idea it was that bad. Caleb told me what happened to his family, but I didn't realize..." she trailed off and bit her lip.

Xavier reached out and gently pulled it free from her teeth. "It was a long time ago, but I still have my other two fathers. It's mostly not knowing what happened to her, but I assume I wouldn't want to know."

Piper licked her lips and then looked up into his eyes. Xavier wanted to stare into the sea-green depths forever. Just being near her eased some of the pain he'd carried around for years. Then she surprised him. Piper threw her arms around his neck and hugged him tight.

He stiffened at first, and then relaxed in her arms, pulling her onto his lap and just holding her. This peace he felt – this was what having a mate was about and he felt it click into place deep in his soul.

Piper was his.

CHAPTER EIGHT

PIPER

Geez, these men – they carried around so much pain and heartache. She was just beginning to understand the world they came from. The blood feud with the crocs had literally torn their pride to pieces and now they were trying to kill the next generation of leopard shifters.

Even if she didn't like her part in it, and wasn't sure how she felt about being a mate – Piper wanted to help Xavier, Caleb, and Niko. There was no reason she couldn't let this thing between them pan out. Because if she were honest with herself she'd never felt quite as content as she did with the three of them around.

And watching the way Xavier and Niko cuddled on the couch together...it was the cutest thing she'd ever seen and had turned her on in ways she'd never expected. Piper had no idea that just the idea of Niko and Xavier kissing would make her so wet she literally had to change her panties.

These guys were teaching her things about herself even she hadn't been aware of. Somehow, it felt like fate.

When she pulled back Piper stared into Xavier's eyes and felt that heat between her legs again. His lips were full and he looked at her like she was some kind of goddess. Her heart beat wildly in her chest and for a moment Piper wanted nothing more than to kiss him.

Having the three of them around had been hard on her emotions, but they also wound her to the point her skin felt tight and there was that heartbeat between her legs pushing her to make a move – to see if it would be as good to kiss Xavier as she thought it might be.

Tentatively Piper leaned forward and Xavier's eyes widened, but he didn't move. He let her take the reins and lead them. Between him and Niko, Piper felt cared for and precious and she wanted that desperately – even if a week ago she didn't care one bit if a man never looked at her again.

She placed her hands on his shoulders for balance and then gently pressed her lips to his.

Instantly Xavier scooped her up, pulling her all the way onto his lap until she straddled him, his hard length pressing against her. Piper couldn't help the moan as he crushed her to his chest. The ache between her legs begged for her to do something about it, but she was lost in the taste of him – that scent of night air on fur. It was wild and intoxicating and she wanted more.

Piper wrapped her arms around his neck and slipped her tongue into Xavier's mouth, desperate for all he had to give – needing to be as close to him as physically possible. Clothes, they were wearing too many clothes.

Xavier's hands went under her shirt, gripping onto her sides like he needed her just as badly as she did him. The feel of his hardness against her had her losing her mind. Piper wanted him now, and she didn't give a shit they were in a library.

"Well, isn't this adorable."

"For fuck sake, demon!" Xavier cursed. But he didn't let her go; instead he wrapped his arms around her and held her even tighter.

Eisheth just chuckled. "Have you called Jess yet, my little queen?"

Piper couldn't help but laugh. It was the most awkward and embarrassing situation she'd ever been in, but it was also hilarious. Eisheth didn't care one bit that he'd popped in and interrupted them. Thank goodness or Piper might have stripped then and there.

She slipped off Xavier's lap and straightened her shirt. Piper had to cross her legs and clench her thighs together to help ease some of that ache. Lord, that boy knew how to kiss. "I haven't yet. Morgan suggested we come here first and Xavier doesn't like the demon hunter."

Eisheth lounged against the table and pulled one of the books closer to him. "I suppose doing some research couldn't hurt, but Jess already knows everything in these books. Why don't you like her, kitty cat?"

It was difficult not to smile at the nickname.

Xavier glared at the demon and crossed his arms over his chest. "It's nothing personal. I don't like witches and I don't like demons. She's something in between. So I'd prefer if she stayed as far away from me as possible."

"Ah, yes, well..." Eisheth inspected Xavier from head to toe and then leaned in to whisper in Piper's ear. "He is *very* well endowed, my little queen. I'd put a ring on it asap."

She burst out laughing despite the blush she could feel burning her cheeks. "I will take that under advisement. Do you have any books you'd personally recommend? I promise to call Jess myself."

"Good, and I rather like this one. Talks about us demons

like we aren't all the same monster." Eisheth handed her a book and winked. "Enjoying your mates?"

Piper cleared her throat and opened the book. "It's really none of your business, perv."

The demon laughed hard at that. "I am kind of a perv. Also I wanted to make sure you had this if you ever needed it." Eisheth leaned forward again and then whispered three words into her ear before he popped out of existence.

"I wonder if the witches know demons can just come and go as they please," Xavier grumbled.

Piper felt her blood cool as she memorized those three words, but she took Xavier's hand in hers and held it like they'd been girlfriend and boyfriend forever. "He gave me his true name," she told him. "So I can summon him if I need to."

Xavier gave her an appraising look. "Why does that demon like you so much?"

The heat of the moment had passed, but Piper felt like they'd gotten closer somehow in more ways than just physically. She grinned at him. "Why, are you jealous?"

That slow, lazy smile spread over his gorgeous face again and he tugged her closer so he could wrap an arm around her shoulders. "Maybe a little."

"I'm a queen, remember? That's why he likes me." Piper opened the book and realized it was in Latin. Well, this wouldn't be light reading.

"You're a queen?" Niko asked, sliding onto the bench on her other side. He studied the way Xavier held her and then smiled. "Well, I know you're *our* queen, but didn't realize you were a literal one."

Piper smiled back. She did feel like a queen with the way these guys looked at her, anticipating her every need. It was easy to see herself falling in love with them.

Even Caleb, if he'd let her. That one was complicated

and...there was a lot of pain waiting for her there. Piper didn't know if it would be his or hers, but she didn't feel ready for it regardless.

"Cleopatra VII is my ancestor," she explained, flipping through the book until she found what she was looking for. "Eisheth says my blood can curse your people."

Niko shared a look with Xavier. "A race of humans that worshipped cats. Yeah, I could see pharaoh's blood being used to curse us. Well, shit."

"Pretty much," Xavier agreed. "But what curse would they even use?"

Piper scanned the page on contracts and shrugged. "Does it matter? I doubt it will be pleasant. Maybe they'd trap you in your leopard form."

There was a lot that could be done with blood per the demon books if the index was any indication. It made Piper a little nervous for the first time since she'd learned Eisheth didn't actually want to deliver her to the crocs.

"So were my eyes deceiving me or were you making out with her X?"

Piper blushed, but didn't take her eyes off the Latin words.

"Yup, she had my lips first."

"Damn, guess I'll have to show her how to really kiss. You aren't always that great at it. You're better at uh, other things."

Piper squirmed in her seat as she tried not to picture what 'other things' Niko was talking about.

"My tongue is pretty magical," Xavier admitted. "You know cats, we're good at licking things."

Piper slammed the book closed and frowned at Xavier, who was too busy grinning at her to give a shit. "Would you rather just call Jessica then?"

Niko scooted closer to her and then wrapped his arm

around her waist, tugging her into his side. "I can smell how badly you want us," he murmured into her ear.

Well, *that* was embarrassing. Piper let her hair fall over her face so she could hide for just a moment, but her heart thundered in her chest and if they could smell her like that, well no doubt they could hear her heart beat as well.

"I'm trying to save your asses," she griped. "But at this point I'm just going to call Jessica since neither of you are interested in studying." Piper wanted them badly, but she also didn't want to be some sacrifice in a spell at the end of two weeks.

Niko pulled back and looked down at her in surprise. Even Xavier's eyes were wide with shock. "You cursed!"

Piper chewed on her lip, annoyed she'd lost her temper. She swiped her hair behind her ear and cracked open the book again. "Yes, well, don't get used to it. Read something and be useful."

Xavier grinned at Niko. "She wants us to be useful. What do you think we could do to be *useful*?"

Niko smiled playfully and opened another book. It was all she could do to keep her eyes on the dang text. These two were going to kill her. "Oh, I'm sure we could think of *something*. You could lick her while I read the Latin books out loud. After all, we both know you can only read English, X."

"We're in a library," she hissed, clenching her thighs together and reading the same line for the hundredth time. "If I caught two students going at it in my library I would kill them. And I *have*. It is not pleasant."

"I really don't think Oscar gives a fuck," Niko admitted. "He didn't even say hi when I came down."

Piper looked up with a frown. "How *did* you get in?"

Niko scooted closer and set his hand on her thigh. "Eisheth left the door open."

Of course he did. The demon liked her mates, and obviously he wanted them together. Piper wondered why that was. Maybe he was just a nosy matchmaker-type. Who'd given her his true name. That little bit of trust had filled her with a weird warmth.

Piper had never really felt like she belonged out in the real world with other people and their dating apps, insta, and snaps and whatever new trend was going on. She never really had friends, female or male. Her father had been her only friend for a very long time. There was nothing wrong with that in her opinion.

Why would she want to hang out with some shallow person who only listened to her so they could have their turn to talk about themselves? There had been a few times with other doctorate students Piper thought she might have found someone she could hang out with, but everyone was so busy with their own thesis.

Then there were those who came just for the Sac State Hellenistic Collection. She'd thought for sure she'd click with someone who had her same interests, but unfortunately she'd been wrong. So Piper had stuck with her dad. While he never really got her intense interest in Ancient Egypt he supported it. He even watched documentaries with her when they weren't in the middle of a sci fi show.

But these three, well at least Niko and Xavier – she felt like it was so easy to be around them. They didn't really push her into doing something she didn't want to do. They were interested in her interests and didn't really care that she was weird and isolated. The only time she went out to socialize was to her Tango classes and milongas.

Piper was stubborn too. She'd gone on Grindr to find a gay partner after the first disaster with her straight one. The relationship had been a hot mess – full of passion and lust just like the dance, but he'd been that way with every woman he'd danced with.

She never permanently partnered with anyone who was into women ever again. It had been a mistake, but one she'd learned from. The dance was an addiction and it was easy to mistake that addiction for tango as one for the person. Her current partner was happily married to a man, and they had three beautiful children.

It was much better that way.

"Shoot," she muttered, pulling out her phone. "I need to text Patrick."

Both Xavier and Niko raised their eyebrows at that. "Your boyfriend?" Niko asked, tightening his grip on her thigh rather possessively.

Piper laughed. "Why, are you jealous?" The same question she'd asked Xavier. These guys were so possessive and intense. It was weird, but she kind of liked it.

"Maybe," Niko murmured against her neck.

It took all her willpower not to lean into that caress. "He's my dance partner. We usually meet up tonight." Niko pressed a kiss to her skin and it made her feel rather breathless.

Xavier leaned an elbow on the table to watch. Those amber eyes of his practically glowed with only the witchlight in the library. "Don't cancel on our account. I'm sure we could take you dancing."

Piper sent the text and then laughed. "It's not just dancing," she told him, ignoring Niko's gentle touches as best she could. "Patrick and I compete as amateurs in tango. The club we go to is for practice and not really for beginners."

Those amber eyes twinkled at her like they did the first time I saw him. "Every time I learn something new about you I'm impressed."

Xavier went back to his book and Niko followed his lead, but both didn't let go of her. Xavier held onto her hand and Niko her thigh. It was difficult to feel worried or unwanted between the two of them.

"So what's it like being a cat shifter?" she asked. Piper felt like they knew so much about her, but she hardly knew anything about their lives at all.

"We all have jobs just like humans do."

That piqued her interest. "Really? What do you do Xavier?" Piper felt a little embarrassed she'd never thought to ask.

Xavier didn't seem to like the question because the smile disappeared from his face, but he answered her anyway. "We all served eight years in the Army right out of high school. Then I went into welding when we came back to Crescent City. Niko went to school and became a teacher. Caleb's family has money and owns most of the original businesses in town. So he focuses on pride business and runs those."

Niko nodded. "I teach at Sunset High. Most paranormals send their kids there. I'm not the only pride member on staff. It keeps our people and the humans safe. Hormones are a bitch to deal with when someone can shatter windows with their mind or turn into a lion."

The shock was almost strange. It was just so...normal. For some reason she pictured them on some kind of commune and isolated from the rest of humanity. "Well, what do you teach Niko?"

Xavier wasn't interested in talking about their lives back in Crescent City anymore and Piper wondered why that was as she turned to face Niko. No wonder she'd felt an instant connection to the quieter of the three men, he was a teacher. He was a lot like her.

"I teach a few subjects, but I prefer math and chemistry."

"Niko was an EOD tech in the Army, diffusing bombs and shit," Xavier explained. "That's why he's so good at chemistry."

Piper studied Niko's handsome face. He was such a sweet, easygoing guy. She never would have guessed he used to do something so dangerous. "Did you all serve in the military for a reason?"

"We needed the training," Niko admitted. "We needed the money for school, and the knowledge on the guns and weapons. Our blood feud with the crocs makes all that necessary. With the witches' help we are able to protect our territory with tech magic. Morgan is the best in that field. We got lucky."

"This says you can kill the demon to get out of the contract," Xavier said, changing the subject. "That sounds pretty easy."

"No!" Piper snatched the book from him and scanned it. "Eisheth is ancient. You're not going to be able to just kill him."

"Babe, you have his summoning name. I won't hesitate to kill him if it keeps you alive." Xavier was deadly serious and the tone in his voice took her breath away. This man would stop at nothing to keep her safe – to keep her alive. Unlike his mother.

No matter how much she hated the idea – Xavier would go there for her.

As much as she liked flirting with them and as much as she was physically attracted to them that was a level of dedication Piper had never truly experienced outside her relationship with her father. But that wasn't the same thing. That wasn't trusting an essential stranger to do whatever necessary to protect her.

Piper felt herself fall a little more for Xavier. It didn't matter if they were mates. This was something he would do for her, and she found that oddly romantic even if it simultaneously horrified her. "Well, let's exhaust other options first if that's all right with you. This text states we could ask Lucifer to break the contract as the demon's keeper."

Niko slammed her book shut. "Lucifer is Jess's territory. We never deal with him direct. He's a slippery bastard. Worse than the demons with all their fancy words and literal promises. If Jess wants to call him that's on her."

Piper blinked and then coughed as dust rose in the air. Well, she hadn't expected the Lucifer thing to be real. That realigned her entire world view and raised so many questions she didn't think these boys wanted to answer. Perhaps Eisheth would.

"What about another contract to void the first?" she asked.

"Contracts with demons are not on the table." Caleb's deep voice rumbled over her and she jumped. Damn these guys were so quiet. She hadn't even heard him walking up. "We'll have to find another way."

Piper looked up at Caleb and he had his arms crossed over his chest again. It made him look intimidating, but it also made his arms look massive. She licked her lips as nerves fluttered in her stomach. Was he mad at her for the demon thing?

"I suppose I can call Jessica then," she said softly, hoping the suggestion didn't upset him.

Caleb glanced between the three of them and he sighed. "Yes, let's call the demon hunter. Oscar said you could take some of these home," he said, waving at the books on the table. "But if you don't bring them back by the end of the month they curse you with bad luck or something ridiculous like that."

"I get to take some home?" Piper couldn't believe it. She started stacking books like crazy and Xavier and Niko only chuckled when she went to the demonology section, grabbing anything she thought she could use.

"There might be a limit on books," Niko teased.

"You may take up to ten," Oscar said as he walked up to them with his hands clasped behind his back. "Morgan called to inform me she found a talisman you might need and to invite you to Sacramento's Golden Coven's Beltane Ball in two days so you may retrieve it."

"You guys have a ball?" Piper couldn't believe all this had been just under the surface. How had she missed so much? Now that she knew about it, she wanted to learn everything. "I want to go."

Caleb frowned at the witch and looked like he was about to say no.

"Please?" she asked.

That stern expression softened just a little and Piper could see the sadness hiding behind his intensity. "Going to a witches' ball is not safe. They are neutral and so invite all kinds. At this point in time I wouldn't feel safe with you going without me. So if you're okay with having me as your date, then you can go."

Oh goodness. Piper felt her heart clench like it had when he'd told her about his family. Maybe Caleb wasn't the scary guy he always showed her, distant and aloof. Maybe he was just as lonely as she was.

Piper didn't look at the other two and held Caleb's gaze. "I'd be happy to have you as my date."

The look of surprise on Caleb's face was something she

didn't quite know how to deal with. Maybe he didn't think she'd agree. Piper wondered why he thought she didn't want to go with him. Was he just as confused about their non-relationship as she was? Well...maybe the ball would give her a chance to find out what he really thought.

CHAPTER NINE

PIPER

Piper wore nothing but a towel as she surveyed her closet, trying to figure out what to wear for the witches' ball.

After she had closed up the library on Saturday and the guys had taken her demon books for her, they'd gone back to her apartment – alone. But no one had made a move. Instead the four of them had sat on her couch and watched the original Star Wars trilogy all night which surprisingly had been Xavier's suggestion.

It had been nice to say the least. Niko cooked this time, and even though Caleb was slightly apart from them he still sat on the couch with Cat Solo watching everything from his cat tree. It was progress. And Piper wasn't really sure what she thought about that.

Then they'd spent the last two days just hanging out on her days off. Piper read four of the five demon texts while making notes. The guys made sure she ate, slept and took the occasional break.

When she wasn't reading Xavier had her teaching him all

about Star Wars. They'd watched most of the movies and the TV shows while Niko and Caleb participated, though Niko was the only one who would give his two cents on the story.

Despite how hot and heavy they'd gotten in the library no one did more than snuggle her. She would watch TV with one of the three on either side. Sometimes they touched her and sometimes they didn't, but when she fell asleep she sprawled across them which was a bit embarrassing when she woke up.

They were taking their time with her and she could hardly stand it. Finally it was the Beltane Ball and she felt like she was going to burst from the desire she could feel growing until she was ready to rip their clothes off.

It was progress. Piper was no longer opposed to the idea of them even if the word 'mate' was a bit scary. Did she want there to be progress though?

These three men knew they had to share her. They planned on it and had no problem with the idea. If Piper were to be honest with herself the idea of three men falling all over themselves for her was incredibly tempting. But Caleb didn't seem to be trying to get to know her – just keep her alive.

What did that mean exactly?

Well, she planned to find out at the Beltane thing. Piper wondered what someone would even wear to a witches' ball. She supposed she had plenty of options from her competitions, but she also didn't want to be overdressed. Flicking through her dresses she checked her phone and saw the text from Jessica's...sidekick, partner?

Apparently Jessica would meet her at the ball.

Piper had called her as promised. Neither Xavier nor Niko had wanted to. Piper had been too chicken to ask Caleb to do it so...she supposed it had been educational to say the least. A demon hunter...who was friends with a demon.

This Luca guy had answered the phone and said they'd been expecting her call and that Jessica was already on her way to Sacramento. So that had been easy enough.

Piper had spent most of the day reading to distract herself. The guys had mostly left her alone, doing their own thing. Each of them had already done their daily work out and it was something to see when they lifted weights on her balcony or came back from a run all sweaty.

Then at some point Caleb had left saying he needed to go rent a tux so that gave her some indication as to what to wear at least. Even if no one else was fancy, her date would be.

Her date.

Goodness, the idea of going out on a date with Caleb made her so incredibly nervous even if it was just so she could get a witch talisman and meet up with the demon hunter. It felt like more than that to Piper. She wondered if it did to Caleb too.

She tilted her head and studied the options one more time. Thankfully she'd done her hair and makeup first. Her lipstick she'd saved for last after she knew what color she'd be wearing.

"I brought you something," Niko said.

Piper tightened her grip on the towel and tried to ignore how naked she was underneath. She turned to Niko and took the glass of wine from his hand. "Thank you, I really needed this."

He chuckled and flopped onto her bed like he'd been doing it all his life. "I know. I can smell your nerves."

She drank the wine and nearly finished the glass in one go. "I don't know what to wear," she confessed. For some reason Piper felt Niko would be better suited to this dilemma than Xavier would.

"You plan on wearing that necklace again?" Niko asked,

nodding to the scarab around her neck. She hadn't taken it off once since she'd put it on...just in case.

Piper shrugged one shoulder and finished the wine, setting the glass gently on the top of her dresser. "Yes, it makes me feel safer for whatever reason."

"It probably has real magic," Niko mused. "Show me your favorites?"

So Piper pulled out her three favorite dresses – a black one that was surprisingly comfortable but sexy, a red one that always looked great against Patrick's suits, and then the beautiful green one.

"Definitely the black," Niko said. "It's very slinky."

Piper laughed and put the other two back. "It is slinky, and a bit risqué," she admitted, showing him the high slits that practically hit her hips. It made some of the more flashy moves easier. But the real beauty of the dress was the halter top, long, black lace sleeves, and the completely open back.

Niko grinned. "I hope you guys have fun."

She frowned and went into her bathroom, leaving the door open only a crack so she could still hear him. No doubt Niko would be able to hear her even with the door closed. "You and Xavier aren't coming?"

"Not officially," he told her. "We'll be outside for backup. Witches only gave us your invitation and a plus one."

For some reason that made her even more nervous. Piper trusted Caleb to keep her safe, but she also didn't really know how to act around him. Not to mention they were going to be in a new place in a world with people she didn't yet understand.

Though those books she'd been reading had been extremely enlightening.

There weren't many ways to void a demon contract. Sure, there was probably a clause in the contract in case the crocs wanted out. They could re-summon Eisheth and renegotiate the terms of the deal. But that didn't help her – there was no motive or reason for them to void the contract unless threatened. Piper didn't know what it would take for them to do that, but she could suggest it to Caleb.

Then there was the option to kill Eisheth. But Piper refused to go there no matter what Xavier said. There had to be another way, like Jessica and her connection to Lucifer.

There was also the loopholes demons could take advantage of, but Eisheth had said a witch had helped bind him. So unless she was to see the contract herself there wasn't much she could do there. Piper had two other ideas though. She could try to make a contract with Eisheth to protect her which would come into direct conflict with his current contract.

Or the spell to break a binding.

And if neither of those worked...Piper had one more idea up her sleeve, but Niko and Xavier wouldn't like it. Caleb would outright refuse. But it was her life...and theirs. She didn't want to know what the crocs would do with her blood and she certainly didn't want to die to find out.

She tied the neck of her dress securely and adjusted the tight fabric so nothing would fall out. Then she used fabric tape just to be safe. Thankfully she'd never been big in the boob department, but she'd learned the hard way that it didn't matter when it came to dresses – especially with dancing.

Missing her normal *milonga* had been hard. Piper was used to a schedule. But Patrick had understood without pressing for an explanation. Though inviting the boys had crossed her mind, if only to see them at a tango dance, completely out of their element for once. Patrick certainly would have enjoyed the three of them.

Would Caleb have even gone?

Piper slicked on her darkest, reddest lipstick and checked her eyeliner one last time. Simple, elegant, and dressed up enough for an event without being over the top. She pinned a stray curl up and then sprayed one last time to make sure the updo wouldn't fall out.

"So why do you like to dance?" Niko asked from her bedroom. "I mean it's great, but it just doesn't seem like you."

When she came out he was lounged across her bed with multiple shoe options. It made her smile to see him so comfortable in her space with tango shoes all over the place. Somehow it didn't make her feel weird, which she'd been afraid of when she first heard they would be staying with her for her own protection.

She climbed onto the bed with him and Niko couldn't look away from her red lips. He handed her a pair of shoes without once breaking his stare. Piper took the red shoes with straps and buckles that matched perfectly.

"Thank you," she murmured. "These are my favorite."

Niko blinked and looked up into her eyes once more. "So why dance, and why tango out of all of them?"

Thankfully the shoes gave her an excuse to turn away. It was difficult to talk about and Piper never really had to before. No one else had gotten close enough and she and her dad had an unspoken rule to never speak about the subject.

"My mother died right after I was born from pre-eclampsia," she admitted. "It's curable if caught in time, but no one knew. She passed away only a day after I was born, leaving my father with a brand new infant." The buckles clicked into place and Piper started on the other shoe.

Niko must have sensed her discomfort because he placed a hand on her lower back, but said nothing. Surprisingly the contact helped and she took a deep breath to continue. "It was hardest on him I think. He was heartbroken and drowning in grief with a tiny baby whereas I never knew my mother, so I could never really miss *her*. I did miss the idea of her though."

The second shoe was giving her difficulty and Piper just gave up and turned slightly so she could face Niko.

He sat up and took her foot in his hand, gently doing the buckles for her. This man was so incredibly easy to talk to, so sweet – he made her want to pour her heart out to him. The touch on her bare ankle wasn't sexual, but caring.

Piper blinked back tears. "When I became a teenager things weren't easy. My poor father is so...unmodern I suppose. He knew nothing about periods and female hormones or what to expect. I didn't have friends either and most of our extended family is back in Greece and Macedonia. I didn't have any aunts or cousins to help me. It was the first time in my life I felt the loss of my mother – a woman I didn't even know. I refused to go to school."

She searched his eyes and there was no judgement or disgust there. Niko truly wanted to know.

Without making a single noise Xavier appeared in her doorway with an opened bottle of wine and two more glasses. He handed one to Niko and refilled hers before settling everything on her dresser. He handed Piper her glass and then quietly started putting her shoes and dresses away.

Piper watched him with a sad smile. She supposed he'd been able to hear everything from the kitchen and she wasn't sure if she should feel guilty for not thinking to include him in the conversation, but he didn't seem to mind. So she shrugged and pressed on.

"Dad didn't know what to do so he took me to see a therapist. She helped me through a lot and after a few months my life seemed almost normal again and I was happy, but there was something missing. She told me it was in my nature to be anti-social after seeing how much I preferred to spend time with my dad and to study."

Xavier sat next to Niko and they both sipped at the wine. It reminded Piper of her own and she drank at least half of it. She would have to teach these boys how to pour a proper glass of wine.

"Your therapist suggested you take dance?" Xavier asked.

She shrugged one shoulder and took another sip. "Not exactly. She suggested I find something – anything to get me out of the house, to socialize with real people, and the challenge was to find something that would require I build a relationship with someone – if only temporarily."

Piper never really understood why she had such a hard time trusting people. It didn't really make sense as she'd never been hurt or lied to in the past, except for her ex-boyfriend – but that had been after her mental breakdown.

Her therapist had suggested it had something to do with the fact her mother had died so suddenly – that she knew nothing was forever and therefore why build anything at all? It made sense in a way; though sometimes Piper felt stupid for reacting like that to something she hadn't truly experienced herself.

"I wasn't really interested in team sports. The idea of getting to know so many people..."

Niko squeezed her ankle reassuringly and she smiled at him gratefully. These two, Piper felt herself opening up to them more and more, letting them into her world as they showed her theirs. She'd never experienced anything quite so beautiful before – it was like learning your dance partner, but there was a different depth to it that made her shiver with trepidation and longing.

"Dance seemed like something I could enjoy without too much commitment," she explained. "I spent three days straight watching dance videos – everything from ballet to the waltz to contemporary to hip hop. I saw every stupid dance movie that existed and only one dance really spoke to me."

Xavier pulled her across the bed, careful of the wine. "So you picked something quietly passionate – almost violent in its expression?" Those rumbling words took her breath away.

Piper was pressed up against his chest with Niko at her back and her heart started pounding. Hearing something so... viciously poetic come from Xavier of all people wound her up tight.

"I did," she breathed. For so many reasons this dance called to her.

Xavier took her glass and Niko tugged Piper over so that she rolled onto her back. "Before Caleb has you kneeling at his feet, I want to taste you," Niko told her.

Then his lips were on hers, his tongue in her mouth, and his hands were all over her. His kiss was quiet desperation and far more aggressive than she would have expected from him. Niko took her mouth with his and gripped her hip with unapologetic strength. It almost hurt, but not quite. The feel of his teeth on her lips made her groan into him and then suddenly Xavier was kissing her neck while she pressed into Niko.

This was something she'd never thought she'd actually get to do. Piper had fantasies, but she was so busy with everything else that sex and boyfriends weren't something she'd even been interested in for a long time. And suddenly she wanted two instead of just one.

Maybe even three.

That thought pulled Piper out of her desire and she sat up, breathing hard. "I don't understand how this mate thing works," she told them, scooting off the bed. Checking her hair in her full-length mirror she saw her new lipstick had held up to the test at least. Nothing had smeared or moved at all.

"You can ask us anything," Niko said, leaning into Xavier as if they'd done it a million times before.

She reapplied her lip gloss and eyed the two of them. "Are you two mates as well?"

Xavier chuckled. "No, we're just really good friends who occasionally find sexual comfort in each other. Most cat shifters are extremely free with non-sexual touch and affection. When the males are mated to one female, sex can and does occur between them at the female's discretion. If you don't want us touching each other without you – that's up to you. And we haven't since we found out."

Piper glanced between the two of them and felt herself getting flushed as she thought about Niko on his knees before Xavier. She didn't really know how she felt about that. She needed more answers. "Well, there are three of you, not two. How does Caleb fit in? I'm not even sure he likes me as a person."

Niko grimaced and shared a look with Xavier. "Caleb is our Alpha and has been since he was fifteen. We've never been close with him like that. I couldn't tell you how he feels or what he thinks – you'd have to ask him yourself."

Xavier got up, shaking his head. "Caleb honestly doesn't have a say in what you do with any one of us. You are the center of this triangle, not him. What you say or do with us romantically goes. Now he is Alpha so there are some grey areas where he can overrule your wishes for your safety – such as escorting you to the ball himself." He took her empty wine glass and kissed her on the cheek. "Just talk to him. You out of all of us have the best chance at getting through."

Piper fixed her hair one last time and tugged her dress just right. "Can he deny me as a mate?"

Niko's eyes softened. "No gorgeous, it doesn't work like that. But he could be mated to you and you him without either of you being very close. Personally though, I think he just needs some alone time with you to open up. Tonight should be perfect for that."

Both of them left her room and Piper felt those nerves come back and now she was feeling wound up, like her skin was too tight. She brushed her fingers over her lips and then checked her shoes. Niko and Xavier knew exactly what to do with her; how to touch her to get her begging for more – but before she decided what she wanted from them all...Piper had to talk to Caleb.

It would be fine. It was just a witches' ball. She would be okay. Piper needed a little confidence booster was all. Arching her back she popped up on the balls of her feet and flicked her arm up, her other hand on her hip, for a moment she inspected herself in the mirror to make sure her form was perfect, her arm dramatic enough. Then she tilted her head and did a little adorno, sweeping her foot out in a half circle.

Well...at least her posture was perfect. The emotion that was supposed to be there was missing. Piper was far too nervous to let herself go like she normally did.

There were mutters from the living room and she caught Caleb's deep voice among the other two. Her stomach flip-flopped nervously. It would be all right, she told herself again, trying to make it convincing. By the end of the night she would get an answer out of Caleb, one way or another.

She grabbed her purse on the way out and then stopped dead in her tracks when she saw Caleb standing with his back to her, explaining something to Niko. Then Niko nodded her way and Caleb turned.

Piper hadn't needed to see him from the front to know how amazing he would look. The tux somehow caressed his shoulders, as if the fabric couldn't quite get close enough to his body, and damn it all to hell she felt the same way.

His gaze went to her as though drawn by magnets. Those green eyes snagged on her red mouth and then traveled all the way down to her red shoes. The slow look up and into her eyes had her heart beating wildly and knowing everyone could hear it – she blushed, but refused to look away.

The man was practically a god. He cut a devastating figure in that tux with the perfect shoes and a trim beard that followed the line of his jaw into a goatee. Piper really liked the blond on him for some reason and the close cut hair. It was barely tamed with a tiny bit of gel, brushed forward, but it was so short it did what it wanted for the most part. It made her want to bury her hands in his hair and see if he tasted as good as he looked.

Well.

That thought had certainly surprised her. "Are you ready to go?" she asked. There was that shy Piper she knew so well, voice quiet and unassuming. Caleb intimidated her and she didn't feel as comfortable with him as she did the other two.

Xavier came out of the kitchen with a strange-smelling metal ball. "Niko and I have all the weapons packed up."

Caleb still hadn't looked away from her, but he nodded. "Yes, we should head out."

Piper knew it wasn't a real date, but still she'd hoped he would maybe act like it was. Instead Caleb let her walk by him and out the door without once touching her, or offering her his arm. She buried the twinge of hurt down deep.

She'd make him talk to her – Caleb couldn't avoid the subject forever.

CHAPTER TEN

PIPER

The ride to the event had been agonizingly silent. Niko and Xavier didn't bother trying to fill the silence either. This was her night with Caleb and they had to figure this out before she got in too deep. Already she was thinking of inviting them camping with her and her father in the summer – if she wasn't a demon sacrifice by then.

"We're going to the Grand Ballroom?" she asked, craning her head to look at the massive building.

"Yes, that's where the witches formally celebrate Beltane. They've already performed their rituals on the first of May, but everyone likes a party," Niko told her.

"They just...celebrate it out in the open?" Piper asked, watching how Caleb pulled up to the valet parking. They were really going into Sacramento's Grand Ballroom. Lord, this was a bit more surreal than she'd expected – though Piper had no idea what she thought it was going to be like.

"Freedom of religion," Caleb said. "Most people get them confused with modern Wiccans. It's not always the same thing and there are spells on the ballroom tonight to keep those uninvited away."

At least there was that, but the flashing lights and banner stating the Golden Coven's 83rd Annual Beltane Ball made Piper nervous. Had she really not noticed all these years she'd lived right here in this city alongside them when they were so blatant about their events?

She felt kind of stupid.

Piper had been so busy staring at the sign she hadn't realized everyone else had gotten out of the truck until her door opened and she nearly fell out.

"Careful," Caleb said softly, catching her before she made a fool out of herself.

Blushing again she took his offered hand and let him help her out of the car. This was what she'd been hoping for. This small bit of chivalry and romance, but it could just be good manners. Piper didn't know Caleb well enough to tell the difference. He could be this way with every female out there.

For some reason Piper hated the idea of him taking another girl anywhere. He was her mate after all. "Have you ever been to one of these before?" she asked, waving goodbye to Niko and Xavier.

Niko mouthed 'good luck' and then the two of them disappeared around the corner of the massive building.

Sacramento's Grand Ballroom was an ode to the Ancient Greek Parthenon with its columns and rectangular shape. Somehow that felt ominous on a night she was about to see a demon hunter for advice on how to keep her pharaoh's blood out of the hands of those who wished to obliterate the lives of her mates.

Well, Piper glanced at Caleb as she waited for his answer. She felt a bit too possessive over three men she hardly knew, but then again magic and fate never really made sense to begin with. And what were emotions and the mate bond but a bit of the same magic?

Caleb led her up the steps and there was no one there to open the doors or check their invitation. He just stopped before them and Piper felt a brush of an invisible *something* against her skin. Then the doors opened on their own, creaking slowly. It made her breath catch and without thinking she took a half-step closer to Caleb.

Nothing signified the end of the human world with quite so much flair as magical doors opening into black nothing. Fog even drifted over the stone steps, but still she couldn't see inside. The moment they stepped over the threshold though... lights flared and the darkness glittered – becoming a gothic underworld steeped in magic.

Piper could feel it crackling against her skin like electricity, tasting her energy and getting to know her in intimate ways. It wasn't a sensation she enjoyed. She was practically flush with Caleb's side as they walked into the magical wonderland with twirling acrobats hanging over the dance floor, pits of fire, buffets groaning with colorful food, and the most ethereal servers who whisked through the crowd with eerie grace.

As if they could all smell her humanity the witches turned as one to inspect her. If she could get any closer to Caleb she would – as if his shifter scent would cover hers.

"It's all right," he murmured, pressing a hand to her lower back to move them forward. "You are a guest and my mate. No one will harm you."

For the first time since finding out, Piper felt relief at the word 'mate.' He was right of course – witches were neutral and nothing else could hurt her with the pride's Alpha at her side. Even if she wasn't sure he liked her, she knew without a doubt Caleb would keep her safe.

EMMA DEAN

Piper was offered a glass of something purple and sparkling with a stick in it that looked like rock candy. The drink was so pretty she reached for it on instinct. Caleb took her hand and turned her in the opposite direction.

"Don't drink anything here," he muttered, eyes flicking everywhere. "I also suggest you don't eat anything either. You don't know what it might be spiked with."

"I wish you would have told me," she said. "I'm starving."

Still he didn't look at her. "We'll grab something on the way back."

"Or she could have this," a feminine voice said from behind them.

Piper turned around to see a woman who she'd guess was a witch even if she'd seen her walking down the street. It wasn't anything so obvious as a pointed hat or some such thing. The woman exuded this confidence and had a mystical kind of aura. The energy around her felt alive.

She stared as she accepted the plate of food and the glass. Caleb sniffed the air, it was subtle, but it was there. He nodded and she took a bite of the finger food. It was delicious of course and like nothing she'd ever tasted before. The sparkling wine was fruity and light.

"Thank you," Piper said.

"I'm Circe," she said in that strangely seductive voice. "Morgan told me to give you this."

Caleb took the talisman from the witch and Piper had to lean over to see it, catching a whiff of Caleb's night-on-fur scent as well as some kind of spice – clove? Whatever it was it was delicious.

"It's a modified hexagram," Circe explained. "If you wear it, it will protect you from lesser demon or ghost possession, but I believe Morgan wants you to have it for this inscription here," she said – pointing to a nearly invisible etching. "Keeps you grounded to this earth and plane. Demons can't pop you in and out."

Caleb put it over his neck first and then when nothing happened he gave it to Piper. She tucked it gratefully under her dress after some maneuvering. "Why does Morgan care so much what happens to me?" she asked. "I've never even met her."

Circe flashed her a dazzling smile. "Morgan is the strongest witch in a generation. Stronger even than most coven leaders. No one knows her true purpose yet – but she does have some Sight. She's been right about certain future events and so we listen. If you need to be protected there's a reason – and one much bigger than the end of the Klamath Mountain Pride."

With a little swirl and flick of her wrist Circe turned and left them to themselves. Piper finished the wine and set the glass down as she tried not to focus too much on what ramifications there might be if the crocs succeeded.

Caleb escorted her down the sweeping staircase and Piper tried to see everything at once, but it was impossible. "They rented out the entire place," she whispered, wondering what else there was to see.

"We have time to walk around a bit, but then we need to meet Jessica on the rooftop," Caleb reminded her. "There should be fewer people up there, though I know it's a favorite for the spell bar."

"A spell bar?" she asked, handing her empty plate to one of the waiters.

"A bar where you can get spelled drinks," he said as though it should be obvious.

Piper shot him a look. Why was he so difficult to talk to?

There seemed to be only one good explanation. "Are you

disappointed I'm your mate?" she finally asked. She had to know.

The strange, unearthly music chose right then to cut out and Piper felt her cheeks heat as people glanced at them. Caleb whipped his gaze to hers and frowned. "How can I be disappointed when I don't know you?"

Well, all right then. She took her hand out of his and grabbed one of those purple drinks. Hell with it, she might as well enjoy the first and probably last time she'd ever be at a witches' ball.

"Do you want to know me?" she asked, sipping the drink as they went up the stairs.

Lucky for Caleb she could keep up with his quick pace even in her heels. She could *feel* his irritation. Was that part of the mate bond or was she just picking up on it like some humans could?

"Piper," he sighed.

"There you are," a sassy voice interrupted.

She looked up and at the top of the stairs was a woman Piper instantly knew was Jessica James. The demon hunter had a long coat on that dusted the top of her chunky-looking boots. The tight, black leather pants didn't really fit in with the scene and neither did the tank top that was one of those weird intricate reconstructed shirts that had wide braided sides revealing a tattoo that went up her ribs.

Jessica was everything and nothing like she expected.

"This pussy cat giving you blue balls? I've heard he's like that." The hunter grinned wide.

Caleb literally growled, deep in his throat. It was threatening enough Piper went up the last few steps to put herself between Jessica and the pride's Alpha. "He can be difficult," Piper agreed. "But I'd rather talk about the demon's contract."

Jessica eyed her from head to toe. "He certainly needs someone like you. Come with me." A jerk of her head and the hunter walked off without looking back. The flare of her coat gave Piper an eyeful of weaponry and what looked like a sawed off shotgun hanging off her belt.

Were those spurs on her boots?

Piper picked up her pace and wove through the garden to the rooftop where a bar had been set up with a quiet area for people to enjoy themselves. Witches lounged on the couches while they were served drinks that smoked and glowed and glittered.

The hunter ordered something that sounded like 'bloody bones' and leaned against the bar to watch the two of them. She didn't comment on the obvious distance Caleb put between them or their strained silence.

Instead she reached over and tapped the talisman underneath Piper's dress. Somehow Jess knew exactly where it was. "This is a good idea. Morgan right? She's a clever one. Well, it'll help but it won't keep Eisheth from putting you on an airplane."

Piper glanced at Caleb and then slipped onto one of the barstools, careful of the slit in her dress. "Can you speak to Lucifer? From what I've read he is the only one who can nullify a demon contract."

Jessica took a red drink from the bartender that looked like it could burn someone alive and downed it like it was nothing. Then she ordered two shots of straight whiskey. "It's a lot more complicated than that, babe."

"Jessica," Caleb growled.

"Call me Jess." She flicked a look at the leopard and then leveled that heavy gaze on Piper once more. "You're some kind of scholar yeah? You study what exactly?"

"The Hellenic Period."

"Right, English please."

Piper didn't dare roll her eyes. "Ancient Egypt in layman's terms."

The two shots of whiskey came and Jess slid one to Piper. "So they had gods for everything right? Well...the paranormal world has many gods – everyone's gods. Eisheth is not one of Lucifer's. Eisheth is Samael's and no they're not the same person. Neither is Satan."

Piper was glad she was sitting down. She downed the whiskey and managed not to cough it all back up. "They're all different people?"

Caleb ran his hands through his hair in frustration. "Can we finish this up? I want to get out of here as quickly as possible."

Jess reached back behind the bar and snagged that bottle of whiskey when the bartender was busy making and enchanting other drinks. She poured more shots and handed one to Caleb. "Loosen up, kitty cat. Your mate's life is in danger. Show some concern."

Caleb stepped forward and got in Jess's face. "I am concerned. I haven't slept since I found out. What do you think I've been doing these last few days?" he demanded in that angry, growly voice that made Piper shiver.

Jess wasn't fazed at all. She threw back the shot and poured another. Then she arched an eyebrow at him, and the sheer audacity and pettiness in that look – Piper threw back her second shot, coughing while she held out the glass for a third.

"Looks like you've been doing everything but taking care of your mate," Jess said calmly.

Piper wanted to laugh, badly. She had to turn away to hide her smile and shared a look with the bartender. Caleb was about to blow a gasket and she could feel that explosive anger radiating off of him.

"I dare you to say that again," he snarled.

"Checking the perimeter isn't taking care of your mate, kitty cat. Now – as for this demon thing. No, Lucifer can't void Eisheth's contract, but he does have the power to complicate things for the crocs. I'll ask him to get in touch with Samael."

Caleb flexed his hands into fists and bared his teeth at Jess. Piper decided now was a good time to stand up and get out of their way. Her heels clicked and Caleb's hand snatched out faster than lightning. He tucked her into his side and then cracked his neck, as if her touch soothed him as much as his did for her.

"I don't want to get into a fight with you, hunter. You're helping my pride and mate. I appreciate that, but get your nose out of my personal business." Caleb wrapped his arm around Piper's waist and the feel of his tux on the bare skin of her back made her lean into him even more.

"So why are you here?" Piper asked. "You could have told us all this over the phone."

Jess smiled at her, ignoring Caleb completely. "I don't know what you know about me, but I'm part demon and part witch, but not really either. It gives me some weirdo abilities that most hate me for."

The hunter slammed another shot. "Visions are one of them. They aren't always clear and I don't always know when they'll occur so they're pretty much useless except on the rare occasion I can see the person's face, hear their name, and see their location. I scried for you Piper Leigh Kostopoulos. I didn't plan to do anything about it because shifters hate me and I usually leave them alone, but Eisheth is a friend of mine and he called in a favor."

The way she said her name reminded Piper of Eisheth – a demon. For the first time since meeting Jessica James, Piper could see the bit of extra her mask of humanity camouflaged. Piper blinked. "So what do we do?"

"You do nothing. I just needed to see you and get this." Jess pushed off the bar, showing the piece of Piper's hair she snagged. "Don't do anything yet, but you have an idea that will work. If I can't break the contract – do that. I'll call you after I've spoken to Lucifer and Samael."

The demon hunter walked back into the ballroom and Piper looked up at Caleb. He watched her go with a glare. "What is she talking about?" Caleb demanded.

The politics and tension between the different paranormal races didn't really make sense to her, but she decided that Jess hadn't said what her idea was aloud for a reason. "Why don't you like her?" Piper asked, changing the subject.

"Demons are chaotic by nature," he said, leading her back into the ballroom when she shivered again. Maybe she was a little cold. "It makes it very difficult to trust them."

"She's not a demon," Piper pushed.

"Close enough."

"Is that why you don't like me, because I'm human?"

"Piper," he said when they reached the main floor. "I do like you."

He led them back into the main event space where it looked like people were starting to dance as the music tinkled through the room. Piper naturally gravitated towards the edge of the dance floor to watch. It was some kind of strange, beautiful waltz.

"You have an odd way of showing it," she told Caleb. The music changed into something slower, something darker... something familiar.

Piper felt it in her chest first like she always did – this strange shift like her heart slowed to match the beat, spreading warmth, radiating it outward until it hit her arms. The instinct to search the room was hard to resist.

"Piper, I don't know how to tell you what you want to hear. I've been Alpha most of my life." Caleb eyed her and slipped his hands into his pockets. "It didn't seem you were interested anyway."

That made her heart clench painfully and she spared him a glance. The music's slow, twisting beat was distracting her. A man caught her eye and she smiled as he approached. A dance would be just the thing to help her relax – figure out what she should say to Caleb, because he was obviously confused and Piper was just as bad when it came to voicing her emotions.

The other man held out his hand for her and Piper stepped forward to accept it. Before she could place her hand in his though, another's grabbed her hand hard enough to hurt. Piper looked up in surprise and was shocked to see it was Caleb.

"She already has a partner," he gritted out. The other man nodded and moved on to the next woman.

Piper glared at Caleb. He couldn't control her like this. "What, I'm not allowed to dance with anyone?"

The way he looked down at her – a flick of his wrist and she instinctually spun out onto the dance floor. She was so surprised she stumbled, but Caleb was there to catch her, dipping her so low she gasped.

"You already have a partner," he told her. His voice was deep and resonated through her at every point of contact. That was when she realized his hand was holding her bare back and it practically burned. Caleb looked into her eyes and all she could do was hold on as he yanked her up and into a close embrace.

Piper's heart beat wildly as she realized Caleb knew exactly what he was doing and he did it with a level of skill that was rare. Following him was effortless. His right arm around her back and his scorching hot hand on her skin had them pressed chest to chest. Piper's left arm instinctually went over his shoulder in the proper position as they stared at each other for a moment.

Caleb took her right hand and stepped forward – in perfect time with the music. His style was slow, close, and they touched everywhere from her chest all the way down her right hip and she followed him without question.

"I'm terrified of losing you," Caleb admitted. He looked down at her with an unreadable expression, but in that moment it didn't matter.

Tango could speak for them in ways that words simply couldn't express. Every note of the song echoed in her blood. Caleb's green eyes bore into her as he led her through the steps – every move was a question, and an answer. He suggested and she followed.

When his hand moved from her back to her hip she knew what he wanted from her, what he needed, and it was nothing to shift, sliding one foot out as he moved them from one end of the dance floor to the other.

"I thought *you* didn't like *me* after what happened in the library," he said quietly as they moved, her cheek pressed to his. Every word was crystal clear despite the music. "Every time I'm near you, or you look at me I can smell your fear."

"I *am* afraid of you," Piper whispered on a turn. "You are like no one I've ever met, but I'm mostly scared that this choice was taken from you and you were left with me – and now I worry I'm not what you want."

Caleb stopped them and he looked down at her for a minute, his expression unreadable. Then he moved.

Each step was dramatic, full of tension, and when his hand pressed against her back she did as she was told – spinning and tangling her legs with his. When he hooked her leg over his hip and lunged into a deep dip with his forehead pressed to hers...

This was what made tango an obsession – an addiction.

Caleb and Piper hadn't been able to talk, hadn't been able to understand one another – not with words. But in one song she knew everything she needed to know about him. He was asking her to trust him, showing her his power as she crossed her leg over her hooked knee and he spun them both across the floor, arms embracing her – promising her he would never let her go, never let her fall...Caleb would lead her through what came next if she would only follow.

He slowed down their movements so she could catch her breath and he leaned into her space, his entire arm across her back and embracing her. "At first I was angry that the universe gave me a human mate," Caleb admitted, his breath tickling her ear and she shivered. "But only because of what happened to my family, to the strong females in my pride. If I couldn't protect them, how could I possibly protect you?"

Piper held his neck and pulled her head back so she could look into his face. "How do you feel now?"

"I'm still angry the crocs won't let this blood feud go, and that now they've brought my unsuspecting human mate into it just so they can curse my pride. But ever since you threw that book in my face I've been in love with you – even if I don't know you very well."

Caleb whipped her into another dramatic dip and she stared up at him with her mouth open in shock.

Did she love him? How could she when they hardly knew

each other? But emotions didn't have to make sense – and they rarely ever did anyways even without things like mate bonds. Tango had taught her that.

As they moved across the floor she didn't have to ask him anything else – not with words. Tango was about power and vulnerability. His body asked hers a question and she answered with a flick of her foot or complicated footwork that intertwined with his before he paused to caress her face and then all the way down her body.

Piper felt it in her blood – in her bones. It was passionate and intimate. Caleb's hips against hers and the slow movements asked her to be patient, to feel what he was feeling – and she pressed as close to him as she could while he did what he wanted with her body.

The song and the dance and Caleb absolutely consumed her – it was like love at first sight – that's what the tango felt like with someone whose body meshed with hers, who dominated her, yet gave her the room to add her own style and flare.

When Caleb spun her out there was a moment as she flicked an arm up and looked back at him, she could see the fire and love in his eyes. The mournful strains of the tango song asked them to pause and then give themselves over to the sensation of fiery passion.

Caleb wrapped her arms around his neck and stepped backward, dragging her forward before whipping her to the side and his strength left her utterly breathless. Never had a partner been so perfect for her – so in tune with her and she with him. He barely had to move his hand for her to know what he was suggesting.

Piper caressed his leg with her foot in a brief moment of respite before he led her in a quick promenade across the floor. The music was compelling and haunting with an unearthly violin she felt really reminded her they were in the paranormal world and not the human one.

Normally the tango was barely restrained passion, but with Caleb – she burned alive with it.

The song ended and he kicked her up in a bit of flair before dropping her into a split dip and somehow she knew that was exactly what he wanted from her without any practice at all. She breathed heavy with her back arched ,looking up into his face as glittering lights above them framed his entire body.

Without even trying he pulled her up and then his lips were on hers, hands in her hair as he led them through a sweet, slow salon tango. Not once did Caleb's lips leave hers as he pivoted them slowly, dragging her foot behind them elegantly. His arms were wrapped around her waist and the proper form had gone out the window as he loved her with his body.

Because that's what it was. She could feel the emotion pouring from him – and it was impossible for his actions to lie to her in this moment, this dance she knew so well.

Caleb slipped his tongue in her mouth and she couldn't stand it any longer. Piper took his hand and led him off the dance floor, telling him to follow *her* this time. His gaze ate her up as he did as she asked – a give and take.

Piper needed him in ways she didn't really understand, but her body was on fire and it burned with a need that had been building for days. And she planned to make him do something about it.

CHAPTER ELEVEN

CALEB

Piper threw a look at him over her shoulder and Caleb felt his blood boil and then rush to his dick.

Ever since he'd found out she tangoed Caleb had been hoping to ask her to dance. It was one of the few things he could do with his body that wasn't destructive. But what was the chance the opportunity would arise before she ended up hating him?

Then the Beltane Ball invite fell into their lap. He would be the first to admit he'd been selfish when he'd insisted *he* be the one to take Piper.

Because it did make him a little jealous to see how easily she'd fallen in with Xavier and Niko – though those two always knew they'd be part of the same triangle. They also didn't hold the same responsibilities he did. The weight on his shoulders was crushing. Caleb was the Alpha of a dying pride and Piper was their first shred of hope in a long time.

She was also a curse.

Fucking pharaoh's blood of all things. Damn witches and crocs just needed to leave him and his alone.

"Where did you learn to dance like that?" Piper asked as she pulled him through the tables.

Caleb yanked back and spun them until her back was against one of the walls in the dark ballroom. The curtains hanging down from the ceiling to give the space that extra bit of decoration hid them from prying eyes. The dancing witchlights made his mate's eyes glitter and glow. He pressed against her, hard as a rock, and nipped her neck.

"I own the best dance school in Crescent City which isn't saying a lot. I opened it after I got back from the Middle East."

His hand slid up her bare thigh – that naughty slit giving him so much room to touch and play. Piper gasped and he could barely keep from groaning. Caleb wanted to rip her dress off and take her now. Dancing with her had been a phantom of what it would really be like to be inside her.

Piper wasn't just a queen, she was a fucking goddess and he wanted to worship her.

Caleb dropped down to his knees and nuzzled the apex of her thighs over her dress. Instantly her hands buried into his hair and tightened. It only made his desire worse.

"We're in the middle of a ball," Piper hissed. "Get up."

So he did. Caleb hooked her knee over his shoulder and then stood, lifting her up with him. The witches always planned for such things with their enchanted food and drink. He ran his hand along the wall while he carried her, still rubbing his face against her. God, she wanted him and Caleb could barely fucking stand it.

There it was. He tapped the orb and a door to a room slid open. It was a special bit of magic that allowed for hidden spaces. After all – the coven owned the ballroom. Caleb wrapped his hands around Piper's thighs, gripping them hard while she pressed against his face, rolling against him while he teased her.

Caleb was the first to set eyes on their mate, and he'd be the first to truly taste her.

Gently he laid Piper down on the bed covered in black silk. She looked shocked to see the room, but didn't question it. Instead those beautiful eyes were round with surprise and anticipation as she watched him.

For the first time in a long time Caleb smiled. It was because of her that he could let go, even just a little. Christ how long had it even been since the last time he'd danced?

He pressed a kiss to the inside of her bare knee and pushed the dress up as he trailed his lips along her leg. Then he knelt on the floor and yanked her towards him. Her tiny gasp, the sound of her heart beating wildly, and the scent of her arousal on the air was exactly what he needed from her.

With a growl Caleb ripped her panties off in one smooth motion, revealing her swollen pussy to him. He couldn't hold back the grin this time and he pounced, licking long and slow from the bottom of her slit to the top. When his tongue flicked her clit Piper moaned and she bucked against him.

Caleb was so hard it physically hurt, but he'd been in real pain before and this was nothing he couldn't handle. He would take his time and enjoy her, making sure she enjoyed him.

He was on his knees before her, worshipping her with his tongue, and Caleb knew that even though he was the Alpha, she was the queen. Queen of the Klamath Mountain Pride sounded fucking perfect.

He spread her legs farther apart, kneading her thighs as he slowly licked and laved, tasting the salty sweetness of her, like coconut milk. It made him want more and he growled as he

EMMA DEAN

sucked on her, listening to her gasps and moans to learn what she liked, what she needed.

"Caleb," she murmured, trailing her fingers in his hair.

His name on her lips nearly made him lose control and take her right then and there. It had been too long since the last time and it wasn't just a quick fuck in a club or hotel like he was used to. Caleb could feel what she felt to some degree; he could smell it filling the room. Not only that, he actually had feelings for her.

It was like the tango, his tongue dancing around her sweet folds, teasing her clit until she writhed beneath him. Her strength was surprising for a human woman when she nearly ripped the hair out of his head as she came for him.

Her screams could only be heard by him thanks to a bit of magic and he relished that more than anything. "Tell me what you want," he growled, licking her one last time.

She was panting on the bed, eyes wide as she looked up at him with her pupils completely dilated. "What?"

Caleb stood and took a step back so he could see all of her. Those red shoes and that magical lipstick...slowly he slipped his jacket off and tossed it on the black velvet chair in the corner. "Tell me." Then he removed his cufflinks. "What you want." Caleb unbuttoned his shirt as he waited for her response, enjoying the way she watched him.

As Alpha he was the most dominant and powerful male in the pride. But the way Piper looked at him – it made him feel powerful in a completely different way.

She bit her bottom lip and hiked her skirt all the way up and over her hips. The sight made his mouth water and Caleb groaned as his dick throbbed. "I want you to make love to me," she whispered. "Show me how you feel."

He could definitely do that.

His shirt went on top of his jacket and Caleb slipped off

114

his shoes and socks. His belt went next and Piper spread her knees apart for him, ready and trusting. He climbed onto the bed and left a trail of kisses from her ankle up her leg and then pressed one to Piper's clit before licking the curve of her hip.

Caleb ran his hands over her silky skin. She wanted him to make love to her – to show her what he couldn't say with words, not like Xavier or Niko could. His hands skimmed over her stomach and breasts until he was leaning over her, untying the top of the dress. Caleb was desperate to see her, to take all of her in.

She let him pull the top down and off her arms so only the necklaces were left. His gaze caught on her dark nipples. Caleb palmed one breast and leaned down to lick the other, being as gentle as he possibly could. Then he ground against her so she could feel how hard for her he was.

Soon he would be buried inside her.

Caleb kissed her breast, still rolling and kneading the other while her hands explored the planes of his chest. The noises she made were the best kind of torture. He kissed the pulse in her throat, feeling the spark of magic from her necklace warm him.

It was nothing to wrap his hands around her waist and lift her up so she was higher on the bed. Then she yanked his pants down and his cock sprang free, pressing up against his stomach – that was how hard he was. Piper looked down and reached for him. Her soft, small hand on his skin nearly made him lose his control again.

But Piper was human; he had to be careful with her. She was more fragile than glass and so precious. Caleb leaned down onto his forearms so he didn't crush her, settling between her thighs. Her sea-green eyes were so bright they practically glowed in the dimly-lit room.

Christ she was gorgeous. He brushed a curl from her face

and rubbed his dick against her, gauging her reaction. Her lips parted and she gripped his shoulders so tight he felt her nails score his back and the pain felt almost as good as her hot pussy against his cock.

"You're my mate, Piper," he murmured, leaning down to kiss that sinful mouth of hers. Her lips were so full and she tasted like nothing he'd ever had before.

This gorgeous woman who was so incredibly sweet, gentle, kind, and unique. Never in his life had he ever met anyone – shifter or human, who had such incredible curiosity about the world, paranormal or not. He never wanted her to lose that wonder.

"And you're mine," she whispered against his lips. "Now put your dick inside me before I roll you over and do it myself."

The dirty talk made him chuckle. Caleb had no doubt she'd follow through, but he needed her underneath him right now. He needed to protect her body with his.

Putting most of his weight on one arm, Caleb adjusted so he pressed up against her entrance and the slight resistance was fucking delicious. He slowly eased inside of her, breathing carefully so he didn't fucking lose it after only one thrust – but damn, she was tight as hell despite how wet she was.

Her groan against his mouth nearly ruined the moment and he gripped her hip tight enough to bruise, trying to keep a fucking handle on the situation, but she was so close already. Her walls pulsed against him, milking him even when he paused to catch a breath.

"Any day now, Caleb," she gasped, looking right into his eyes.

It was too much. He couldn't take any more of her sass. Thrusting the rest of the way into her until he was hilt deep was exactly what he'd needed. Her nails ripped through his skin as she moaned, arching her back into him.

It took everything he had not to bite down on her neck and claim her. Caleb stroked in and out, feeling her tighten around him until she was right on the edge. "Come on baby, come for me again," he murmured against her ear.

"Caleb," she whispered, and then she shattered around him.

The sensation of her orgasm had him roaring, pounding into her until he came violently, filling her completely. She'd taken everything from him and Caleb couldn't be happier. He kissed her again, softer this time and with less teeth. The sensation of her skin against his was soothing.

Caleb never wanted to leave her.

Piper smiled up at him, tracing the line of his jaw, his goatee, and then slid her fingers into his hair. She pulled him down so they were hugging. He was careful to keep most of his weight off her, but the simple act seemed to suck all the poison out of his soul.

The stress he'd carried every day since he was fifteen and named Alpha, the pain tattooed on his heart when his entire family had been burned alive, it all seemed to ease with her little touches and the bond between them.

"I want to see you shift," she whispered.

It was so unexpected Caleb laughed and sat up so he could see her face. He tapped her nose and then couldn't help himself. Kissing her was essential now, like breathing. "You want to see my cat form?"

She nodded and then grinned up at him. "If that's okay."

Carefully he slid out of her and was pleased to see she didn't seem embarrassed, or to regret what they just did.

The room was stocked with all the essentials. Caleb grabbed a warm, wet cloth from the bathroom and cleaned up.

Then he got another for her. She didn't even bother cleaning up or fixing her dress.

"You aren't going to distract me. I want to see you as a kitty cat." The determined glow in her eyes made him grin.

Caleb let out a breath and then shifted, dropping to all fours. Her gasp told him she was intrigued, but not afraid. He prowled around the room, giving her time to see all of him, to see his size and strength. Then he jumped up on the bed and rubbed against her face.

Piper laughed and sank her fingers into his fur. It felt so good he fell to the side, careful not to crush her. Caleb lay out on his side so she could scratch more of him and he watched her with half-closed eyes.

She turned so she faced him and ran her fingers over every inch of him, even the pads of his paws. Caleb had never let anyone touch him in his cat form before and this was oddly sensual – relaxing.

"You're adorable," Piper told him. "Not quite the teddy bear inside my father is, but definitely fluffy and cuddly."

He grumbled at the word 'adorable' and placed his paw on her shoulder. She laughed as it pinned her to the bed and she couldn't move no matter how hard she struggled. "Strong and powerful, but definitely beautiful." Piper traced one of his spots and Caleb stood, shaking himself.

It was a bit much for him and he needed to be able to talk to her.

Suddenly he was naked again and she got up on her knees, running her hands over his legs, his sides, and then they rested on his pecs and the way she looked up at him had his heart pounding. "You're beautiful in both forms, Caleb. Thank you for sharing the other with me."

He traced her bottom lip and wondered how long this would last. Would he be able to save her from the crocs? If he couldn't, Caleb knew it would break him. "I swear to you I'll give my life for yours before I let them take one drop of your blood."

Her fingers tangled in the hair at the nape of his neck and she breathed him in. "I believe you. This mate thing goes both ways though. I can feel it even if I don't understand it. And Caleb, I won't let them hurt you or the pride."

The finality of her statement scared him. Caleb had so much to learn about Piper, but he knew this girl didn't lie. Never once had she tried to hide anything from them. What the fuck would she do to keep that promise?

"We should go," he told her.

Piper kissed him, just a soft peck that left him wanting more. Then she went to the bathroom and started cleaning herself up, fixing her dress, carefully pinning her curls back up, checking her lipstick...if he was lucky he'd get to watch her do this for the rest of his life.

"So tell me," she said, eyeing him putting on his pants through the mirror. "If I were to agree to this mate thing, what would be expected of me?"

Her question made him hot and then cold. Caleb didn't react other than to stop what he was doing. He didn't even look at her. This was dangerous territory and it had to be handled carefully or they could lose her. And she'd asked him of all people. Caleb was shit at using the right words.

"That would be up to you," he said, buttoning up his pants. "But the Klamath Mountain Pride is based in Crescent City, California. We own most of the land around there, plus all the forests and National Parks. The other small prides share borders with us. Most of Northern California and the Sierras are owned by various different ones. Together we all make up the West Coast Pride. Crescent City is where I need to be, where I need my Second, Xavier. And we need you."

The silence that followed was like a knife to the chest, but he let it be despite the panic screaming at him to do something. Carefully he slipped on his shirt and buttoned that up as well.

"Would you need me to get pregnant right away?" Piper paused and then came out of the bathroom. "I mean...is it anything at all like being human? Would we all date, and then get married, and then have kids?"

There was that fucking head tilt again. Caleb loved that little tick of hers. It seemed to mean she'd put emotion away for the moment so she could gather information, process, and understand. Those questions...set fire to a desire he hadn't even known he had. Caleb wanted nothing more than to have her in their life permanently and more kittens in the pride...

He turned away and rolled up the sleeves of his shirt, sitting down to put on his shoes and socks. "Being mated is kind of like the fast track. Mates are stronger than a piece of paper, but some mates do get legally married to benefit from human laws. Although it's usually to the most dominant of the triangle since multiple spouses aren't always legal. We don't have many female leopards any more, but that doesn't mean we'd need to rush into anything. Although, I would love to have more kittens."

That word made her smile, but she wasn't done asking him questions. "And my life here? My dad? Cat Solo?"

Caleb stood and slung his tux jacket over his shoulder. Then he turned to look at her. There wasn't anything for him to read from her at the moment and it was aggravating as hell. "Your father would be welcome within the pride. A good cop would be invaluable to Crescent City. Cat Solo is welcome as well. He could even be our mascot. The logistics of everything would need to be worked out, and would be at your discretion."

Piper took a step toward him and placed her hand on his arm. It relaxed him despite how much this conversation fucking terrified him. One wrong word and he could lose her forever.

"Would you turn me into a cat too?"

His breath caught when she pressed against him and wrapped her arms around his neck. He hadn't expected *that* question so soon. The girl was a researcher though, it made sense. "If you wanted, but it's not required. Any children you would have with the three of us would be shifters."

Piper tilted her head up at him and smiled. "I currently have an IUD so I can't get pregnant, but I'd be willing to consider taking it out in the next year if all goes well. I still have my thesis to complete, here at Sac State. But otherwise most of my ties to this city are my father and my job. If my dad wants to move..." she shrugged. "I wanted to consider this as a serious option and I needed all the information." Piper kissed him softly. "Thank you for being honest with me."

Caleb watched her walk toward the door and then stop. When she looked back he knew exactly what she wanted like they'd been together for years. "I think we have time for a few more dances if you're interested," he told her.

She grinned at that and left the room that was already going through its magical cleanse.

This fucking woman was perfect and Caleb refused to mess this up. He needed to text Xavier, and then maybe it would all work out. It was the first time in his life since the fire that Caleb felt hope.

CHAPTER TWELVE

PIPER

Caleb had danced with her for hours and Piper had enjoyed her first Beltane Ball more than she'd ever admit. It had been dark and beautiful. It was like a twisted fairytale and she'd danced with the prince until she was nearly asleep on her feet.

The stress and the emotional overload from the last few days was just too much. She'd fallen asleep on the way home and didn't remember much after that, but someone had carried her to bed.

So on some level Piper knew she was dreaming because she was tied to a slab of rock with people in hoods surrounding her and not in a bed. The curses weren't so dramatic in the demon books she'd read so her logical side insisted it was a dream, no one tied women to rocks. But dream Piper didn't care what was logical and what wasn't.

She was terrified, struggling against the bonds while a man in a hood with a crocodile snout sticking out came at her with a knife. Jessica and Eisheth just stood in the corner doing nothing while this shifter cut her from neck to navel, slicing her entire body open until blood was all that she could smell and she was choking on it.

When he reached into her stomach Piper started screaming, feeling him root around in her organs, looking for something.

Her eyes flew open and Piper sat up so quick she felt dizzy. Her heart was pounding and it was difficult to breathe. Piper grabbed her stomach, feeling the skin to make sure it was smooth and unmarred.

"Are you all right?" Niko asked from the doorway.

She jumped at the sound of his voice. No, she was most definitely not all right. Piper shook her head and wrapped her arms around herself. It was hard to forget how it felt to be sliced open like that. Whether she wanted to think about what could happen at the end of the two week grace period or not, her subconscious was definitely worried about it.

Niko sat on the edge of her bed and wrapped his arms around her. Piper clutched onto him, breathing in the smell of his skin and his clothes. His touch instantly soothed her and she was able to calm her breathing.

"It was just a nightmare," she whispered, pulling him into bed with her.

There was no way she was going to be able to sleep alone now. If Niko could stay with her, maybe she'd be able to get a few more hours. It was almost dawn if the light in the room was any indication, and Piper was still so incredibly tired.

Niko snuggled under the covers with her and held her close. He didn't say anything, but he rested his chin on the top of her head, stroking her arm lightly in a very soothing, pleasant rhythm. It helped settle the violent, frantic pounding of her heart.

"Will you talk to me about something?" she asked, resting her head on his chest. "Help me forget?"

"Mhm," he murmured sleepily, giving her a little squeeze. "Things in the pride aren't all bad you know. My favorite times are when everyone gets together and we meet up with the other smaller prides for the barbecues. We tend to form up by species, but all are welcome. Klamath Mountain is all leopards but the Six Rivers Pride has others, even foxes. I think out of all the other shifters out there, the foxes are my favorite."

Piper closed her eyes and pressed the full length of her body against his. The more she touched him the better she felt. It helped Niko only wore boxer briefs and she was in just a sleep shirt. There was more skin contact, and she couldn't decide if that was part of the mate magic or if it was just natural human contact helping her relax.

"Why are they your favorite?" she asked. Piper sighed as the last of the adrenaline left her.

Niko rolled onto his back, pulling her with him so he could rub her back. "Mm, I think it's that they're the perfect mixture of dog and cat. They're also smaller than the rest of us, but they're crafty as hell. Don't try and corner one, the whole pack will rip you to shreds before you even know they're there."

"A leash."

"Hm?"

"A group of foxes is called a leash," she told him, trying not to wiggle as his hand brushed her ass.

Niko chuckled. "Why do you know that?"

Piper smiled. "Why do I know anything? I read a lot," she teased.

"Stop that," he said, smacking her ass when she moved

against him. "I'm trying to comfort you and you're making it difficult."

Piper could feel him getting hard beneath her, but she hadn't been planning on saying anything until he smacked her. "It's not my fault," she muttered. "You're relaxing me."

"I'm glad I am." His breath tickled her hair.

"Why else do you like the foxes and not like, a tiger pride?"

"They're just a lot of fun. Tigers are usually called clans, but their prides have other types too. And they're usually pretty annoying. Their animal doesn't like being in a pride as much, but their human side does. Not to mention they have this insane protective streak. The Alpha of the West Coast Pride, meaning all of us – Alpha to Caleb's Alpha – is a white tiger. He's pretty hands off, but he steps in when he's needed."

"Why won't he do anything about the crocs?" Piper asked rubbing her face against Niko's chest while she tried to ignore how hard he was against her and how little fabric there was between them.

Niko sighed. "There are a lot of complicated rules. He can't do anything about you specifically because you're human and unclaimed. If you were a cat it would be different. The rules are to stay away from humans, leave them alone unless there are cases like this where one ends up as a mate. It happens more than you think it would. If you don't leave the humans alone, you end up on a hunter's shit list – someone like Jessica. But we have a Council, and only the Council is allowed to send hunters on assignments – if the hunter agrees to the job. Assassinations through other means have happened before though."

"And this white tiger sits on the Council?"

"Clever girl," Niko murmured, his hands moving to her

hips. His fingers pressed into her skin and he rubbed her against the hard length of him.

Piper gasped when she realized that she wasn't wearing panties, just the shirt. She was wet and ready and desperate to know what Niko felt like. He was so sweet and tender with her. Would he be the same in bed, or would he be as aggressive as his kisses alluded?

"Is there an East Coast Pride?" she asked, feeling flushed when he rubbed her against him again.

Niko grabbed her ass with both hands and squeezed. "Mhm. There's a Plains Pride as well. The other countries have their own setups."

He squeezed *hard* and Piper wanted him to do it again but he trailed his hands up her sides and into her hair, pulling her face up to his. When Niko kissed her it was rough and demanding. He wanted her bad.

Piper sucked on his bottom lip and then sat up so she straddled him. She pulled her sleep shirt over her head with both hands so he could see all of her. Niko groaned and traced one of her hardened nipples.

Niko stripped off his boxer briefs almost as smoothly as she'd taken off her shirt. Piper hadn't expected him to lift her off him the way he did just to set her right on his hard dick. He was positioned so perfectly that when he slammed her down onto him it didn't hurt at all, but the quick stretching was a delicious kind of pain.

Her loud moan made Niko's grip tighten on her hips hard enough to bruise. God, he felt so good and he kept moving her, rubbing against her clit just right as he had her ride him. Piper almost didn't have a choice; it was follow his lead or nothing.

Never in her life had she experienced anything as erotic as Niko staring up at her, moving her against him in a rhythm that had her on the edge before she even realized what had happened.

"He's what you would call a power-bottom," Xavier said, his deep voice washing over them.

Piper gasped at the sudden intrusion. She would have stopped if Niko let her, but instead he kept grinding her against him, lifting his hips in perfect rhythm to drive his cock in farther. Seeing Xavier watch them with his hand on his dick made her lose it. Piper came hard, falling against Niko's chest as it rippled over her in waves.

Her shout of pleasure made them both growl and suddenly Piper was on her back with Niko on top of her, kissing her senseless. When he let her come up for air Xavier had climbed up on the bed too.

Xavier kept his eyes on hers the entire time Niko thrust into her. "Mind if I take Niko while he takes you?" Xavier placed a hand on Niko's lower back and Piper's eyes widened.

Her nails sank into Niko's shoulders and she licked her lips as Niko slowed. "I don't mind," she said. "Although I may be a little jealous Niko is the one who gets the ass-play."

Niko laughed and raked his teeth across her throat. "If that's what you want I'm sure we could arrange it." Then he groaned against her mouth as Xavier spread him, rubbed lube all over his length, and then placed the head of his cock against Niko.

Piper couldn't stop watching. Never had she seen two men together before and it was like watching live porn, but a thousand times hotter. Xavier went slow and Niko pressed into her the farther he went in until she was pulsing around his hard cock, close to another orgasm just from watching the two of them.

Xavier was powerful. The way he slowly entered Niko though told her this wasn't new for them, and he cared about them both to be so careful. Piper knew when he was all the way in because Niko shuddered against her and the three of them took a moment to adjust.

Then they both moved. And it was perfection.

Niko pulled out and then Xavier did. Xavier thrust into him and Niko followed by slamming into her. Xavier pressed hard into the both of them which made it look like they were both fucking her. Piper's back arched and she couldn't get enough of them. She wanted to touch Xavier – have him touch her. She wanted to watch them both come hard on top of her.

"Fuck me harder," she told Niko, gritting her teeth at the slow and steady rhythm. "I want Xavier to watch while he takes you."

"Jesus fucking Christ Piper," Xavier muttered, but the two of them picked up the pace. "You always talk dirty like that?"

Piper's eyes rolled into the back of her head as the tight sensation inside her finally released and she clenched around Niko again. He couldn't hold onto it this time. Niko cursed and slammed into her, spurting his cum inside. The heat of it warmed her and Piper managed to open her eyes so she could watch Xavier pound into Niko.

Their eyes met and held while Niko still pulsed inside. It was too much for Xavier and he roared his release. Piper smiled and reached for him as he panted above her and Niko. He obliged and she gave him a kiss. "That was the hottest thing I've ever seen," she told him.

"I always knew the quiet librarian secretly being a freak was a thing," Niko said with a laugh. "Do you always talk like that in the bedroom Piper?"

"She did with me," Caleb said with a laugh.

Xavier and Niko slid to the side and Piper was suddenly

exposed to Caleb. A very naked Caleb whose broad shoulders filled her doorway and his obvious erection teased her. He stood there for a moment, taking in the three of them. "You guys aren't exactly quiet."

Piper could let this be weird, or she could just roll with it. Now that Caleb was there she wanted him too, wondering how long he'd been there, watching. She reached out a hand for him and gave him a smirk. "Would you even want us to be quiet? You might miss out if we were."

Xavier let out a surprised laugh, but Caleb only smiled. "What do you want Piper?" He took a step forward and took her hand in his.

Oh, there were a lot of things she wanted, but one thing in particular came to mind. She rolled over and got up on all fours, glancing over her shoulder at Caleb. "I want you to fuck me from behind while Xavier and Niko make out."

"Fucking hell, woman," Niko muttered, adjusting his dick.

But Caleb only grinned. "You heard the lady."

Piper loved that all three of them did as she asked, that they were so willing to be at her service, especially Caleb – the big Alpha. It made her feel powerful and strong in a way, and she adored that. She could get so used to this.

CHAPTER THIRTEEN

NIKO

Holy fucking shit. Caleb was going to play with them.
When Niko had first found out that Caleb was going to be their third he honestly thought they'd never share their mate together. He was always down for some time just him and her, but Niko had always known he wanted to share her with Xavier in a thousand different ways.

Why not when he and Xavier were already so comfortable with each other?

But Caleb had always seemed like the kind of guy who would only have sex with their mate on his own, and leave them be when it was their turn.

Niko knew that Piper would open Caleb up at the Beltane Ball. She was pushy when she wanted to be, and she'd pushed Caleb right off the edge to get him to talk to her. And when he'd finally talked she'd seen the real man behind the scowl.

Caleb was beautiful and what Niko remembered of him before the fire...sure he was an Alpha and could be an ass, but he was also the most dedicated, quietly passionate person Niko knew. And here he was...getting the front row seat to this passion.

Piper arched an eyebrow at him and Xavier, and Niko snapped his mouth shut when he realized he'd been gaping. Oh the reality of the sexy librarian was so much better than the fantasy. Caleb stared at her like she might not be real, and Niko knew exactly how he felt.

Sure, this was just sex and they were enjoying each other – no emotions or feelings required, but the bond between him and Piper was getting stronger and the physical touch only strengthened it.

But Niko knew he and Piper had similar personalities, similar interests so it wasn't all that surprising that they'd gotten along so well. No, what had Niko in complete awe of her was the spell she'd put on Caleb. It was like watching a man come back from the brink of death to see Caleb *smile* for the first time in years.

Piper squirmed away from Caleb. "Not until these two are making out," she told him.

The shock he felt the first time she'd boldly ordered them to do as she wished had almost made him come on the spot. And it still shocked him every time she opened that dirty fucking mouth to say something else.

Caleb growled at him and Xavier and it would be almost comical if the golden glow of his cat form wasn't flickering in his eyes.

"Poor baby," Piper murmured, reaching out to caress Niko's face. "You want to watch, don't you?"

Xavier let out a slow breath next to him and the two of them were still as statues. Finally Niko nodded. She tilted her fucking head and Niko would never be able to watch her do that again without thinking of this moment.

He licked his lips when Caleb's large hand spanned her neck and held her so her back arched.

"I suppose that's fine," Piper teased. "Just means you get to do it for me later."

Niko had to grip his dick as it hardened painfully. This... this was enough to shove him head over heels in love with her. Not just because of the way she handled them in the bedroom, but because of the way she had Caleb smiling as he slid into her.

Piper gasped and Xavier groaned. Both of them were stroking their dicks as they watched even though Niko would have sworn he was done for the night after Piper milked him dry.

Then Caleb gripped her neck and pulled her up so her back was against his chest, Niko and Xavier could see everything. He thrust into her without mercy and Piper's eyes rolled into the back of her head as she held onto his neck, the sound of flesh slapping together was driving him crazy. And then Caleb's free hand came around to rub her clit. Niko gritted his teeth.

Their Alpha was powerful and strong, but Niko could clearly see the careful way he held their mate. She was just as precious to him as she was to them, just as special – if not maybe more. Piper was hope, she was the future, and Caleb looked at her like she hung the fucking moon as he kissed and licked her neck.

Niko's speed increased as he jacked off to the most erotic scene he'd ever witnessed in his life. His Alpha and his mate. Watching Caleb – Niko felt closer to him than he'd felt the entire time they'd known each other. They'd served together in the Army, and he trusted him – saw him as a brother. Niko also trusted him as Alpha and knew Caleb would do anything to keep their pride safe.

But for the first time he was seeing the man behind all of that, not the boy he used to be or the front he always put on for everyone. There was still that fear in Caleb's eyes, the desolation that leading a dying pride left, but there was also hope and love. Caleb loved Piper.

Niko groaned as he came, spilling cum all over his hand and stomach. Xavier lost it too and then Piper was screaming as Caleb picked up the pace, loving her body with his almost violently. The roar Caleb let out when he came made Niko shudder to imagine what that would feel like.

He could practically feel what Piper felt in the thick air of her room.

Caleb released her neck and wrapped his arms around her, holding her close while she shivered and slowly came back to them. She smiled sleepily and then turned just enough to kiss Caleb.

Niko wanted more, but they were all exhausted. He made a move to get up but Caleb shook his head and laid Piper between him and Xavier. Then their Alpha disappeared into the bathroom. He came back with washcloths.

He knew it was rude to stare, but this wasn't the same man Niko had known his whole life. One glance at Xavier and he knew he felt the same. They all cleaned up in companionable silence and Niko wondered if Piper would want them to leave, but she snuggled into Xavier with her eyes already closed.

Niko shared a look with Caleb and then moved. He spooned Xavier and wrapped his arm around both Xavier and her. Caleb may not be shy, but he wasn't comfortable with them the same way he was with Piper. So Caleb spooned Piper, but he didn't shy away from their contact either.

Did wonders ever cease? This Alpha practically purred sharing this tiny fucking bed with them, their mate already asleep between the three of them. There was no safer place for her to be.

Niko closed his eyes. He dared a fucking demon to try and take her with all three of them there.

"Niko."

God, he was tired. What fucking time was it?

"Niko." Then there was a little push on his chest.

"Hm?" He cracked an eye open and realized he wasn't holding Xavier anymore, but Piper and they were alone.

"I wanted to ask you something."

Niko closed his eye and rolled onto his back so she could lay her head on his chest. "Go back to sleep Piper."

"If you turn me into a cat, could the crocs still use my blood for the curse or would it be different? Even if it's not, would me being a cat make the Council step in?"

He sighed. "You want me to wake up now don't you?"

She giggled and poked him in the ribs. "Yes. Answer my questions."

Niko grumbled and rolled over so he was practically smothering her. He rubbed his face against hers, against her neck, breathing in her scent mixed with all three of theirs.

"Stop!" she laughed, trying to push him off, but she wasn't really trying. "How are you always hard?"

Niko nipped her throat, but was careful not to break the skin. She was fucking delicious and if he could wake up like this every morning he would be the happiest man alive. "Want to do something about it?" he teased.

"I want an answer to my questions."

Niko took her wrists and pinned them above her head. She wasn't trying to get away so he wriggled in between her legs so that he was comfortably pressed against her. "We could claim you and turn you into a shifter. Then you would be officially under Samuel – the Alpha of the West Coast Pride, but it's not a quick process." He licked her throat and then traveled down to nibble on her breast.

Her gasp was music to his ears. "Why not?"

Niko grumbled and moved further down so her breasts were at the perfect level to suck. "You have to register with the pride, file the paperwork, and then once it goes through Caleb can send a request to Samuel." Then he pulled her nipple into his mouth.

Her fingers tangled in his hair and she made a soft moan. "How long does that take?"

Niko looked up at her, annoyed. "Could take a week, could take longer. It's not always the same. Depends on what the West Coast Pride Alpha has going on. Do you want to keep talking or would you rather I do something else with my mouth?"

She laughed and wiggled under him. He could smell how aroused she was already. "We can't do both?"

"Babe, I'm not *that* skilled." He kissed one breast and then the other, moving slowly down.

"Okay, one last question," she murmured, eyes closing in pleasure. "Could they still use my blood if I was a shifter?"

Niko kissed her belly button and kept going, sliding his fingers down and over her clit before parting her slick lips. "I would have to ask Morgan, or talk to a pride doctor. I don't know anything about that."

Then he pressed his mouth to her center and her groan as she lifted her hips to give him better access was exactly what he wanted. Niko was done talking. He wanted to taste her until she came in his mouth.

He licked long and slow, tasting her, diving into her, letting her ride his face as he sucked and nibbled until she was shaking beneath him, practically ripping the hair from his head as she came. Niko flicked her clit with his tongue as she settled, panting.

"See, much better than talking."

Piper smiled and stroked his hair, eyes closed again. "This isn't weird for you guys?"

"What's weird is you cussing," Xavier said, bringing in a tray of food. "Didn't think I'd ever hear you use the word 'fuck' in my life."

Niko laughed and grabbed one of the orange slices. He was still naked and so was Piper, but Xavier was freshly showered and dressed. "Yeah, didn't expect that either."

"Only in the bedroom," she said, blushing despite being completely naked and wet from what they just did. Christ she was adorable.

"I'm not questioning it," Xavier clarified, giving her a sweet 'good morning' kiss. "Just commenting. I love hearing you talk dirty."

Piper cleared her throat and reached for the coffee. "Thank you for this. Where is Caleb? Checking the perimeter again?"

Niko snorted and adjusted. Damn, his dick was still hard as a rock.

Piper glanced at him and grinned over her mug. Instantly his heart rate accelerated as he wondered what dirty thing she was thinking. "Need some help?" she asked.

He desperately wanted to say yes, but he also didn't trust that gleam in her eye. "I'll survive," Niko told her.

Piper arched a brow and then looked at Xavier. "I think Niko needs some help."

Holy fucking shit.

Even Xavier raised his eyebrows in surprise. "You want me to suck him off?"

Just the words made Niko harder and he groaned, pressing his face into Piper's stomach.

"You did say cats were good at licking things."

Niko laughed with Xavier. Somehow that little teasing comment had come back to bite them in the ass.

"What, you don't like to do that?" Piper asked. "Niko may be a power-bottom, but he needs relief too."

Xavier's smile widened and he removed the tray from the bed. Piper sipped her coffee and her eyes sparkled as she watched Xavier grab Niko's ankle and pull. Then he flipped Niko over and looked up at Piper. "With you around we all need relief constantly," he told her, getting down on his knees.

Niko breathed hard and looked down at Xavier. The more dominant and straighter of the two of them, Xavier had never gone down on Niko before. Ever. A hand job was no big deal, but the man had never been that intimate with him before.

The second his warm mouth touched him Niko threw his head back and cursed. Xavier may never have gone down on him before, but he knew exactly what he was fucking doing. He sucked him so hard and so fast Niko barely tapped his shoulder in time.

Xavier stroked him as he came and Niko could have sworn there were stars. Fuck. He'd never experienced anything like that before in his life, not even with a woman.

Piper smiled like a cat that got the canary and sipped her coffee again. "Your turn, Xavier." She set the cup on the nightstand and crawled over to him.

Then her alarm went off and they all froze.

"Mother trucker!" Piper scrambled off the bed and grabbed her phone before running into the bathroom. "I'm going to be late for work!"

Niko looked at Xavier and busted up laughing. To his credit Xavier smiled and got up off the ground. Then he wrapped his hand painfully in Niko's hair, twisting and pulling him forward. The kiss was rough and dominating. Xavier shoved his tongue into Niko's mouth, taking what he wanted.

"I liked that, but I'm still the dominant one," he growled at Niko.

When he released him, Niko grinned up at his best friend. "Whatever you say, man. But between the two of you I might just die of dehydration." He got off the bed and went to join Piper in the shower.

Was this what it was going to be like for the rest of their lives? Niko wiped the blood from his lip where Xavier had bit him. God he hoped so.

CHAPTER FOURTEEN

PIPER

Xavier flipped a page in the book he was reading and she glanced at him for the thousandth time. Her shift was dragging and Piper just wanted to close the library already so she could scratch the itch that had been bothering her ever since she'd watched him suck Niko so hard and fast he came in under a minute.

That took skill.

But they hadn't had time for her to do anything about the raging desire she had after watching that. She had work. Then Caleb said Jess wanted to meet with him and Niko was outside the library making sure nothing tripped his tech magic up.

So it was just her and Xavier. Who was more distracting than she thought he would be.

Most of her shift she'd spent reading demon books and helping a student when they needed it. At this point in her research she probably knew almost as much as a witch or a hunter about demons. The texts were somewhat repetitive, and some were just some kind of demon genealogy.

It was helpful to know who ruled which demons, but it didn't help her with demon contracts or breaking one. The books just stated over and over that the demon was the only one who could use the loophole, and the original summoner the only one to break the original contract, though it wasn't advised.

Most contracts ended in the death of the summoner to be honest. Piper didn't know why the crocs were so desperate. What was it that made them so relentless?

"Could you ask Oscar for more recommendations?" Piper asked, closing the book when she finished. Now she knew more about Jewish demons than she ever cared to know, and still had no more answers than the day before. She should really be reading up on the croc and leopard history, but she was nervous to go down and peruse.

Piper chewed her lip and glanced at Xavier again. It was hard to forget the way he looked on his knees that morning, or the way he'd taken Niko on top of her. The only thing that had helped her get her mind out of the gutter was reading.

"Isn't this like the fifth book you've read? How do you read so fast? This one isn't even in English," Xavier said as he looked the ratty book over.

She shrugged and glanced at the other books. "I read fast, and once I get used to the language again, I can read just as fast as I can in English. None of these are going to be able to help us." Piper tossed the other two on her desk and sighed.

"We don't *throw* demon books," Xavier gritted out. "Some of them are practically sentient and could take offense."

She ran her fingers over the books lovingly, silently apologizing. "I like reading them, but there is no answer we don't already have to this problem. In a week Eisheth is going to have to take me to the crocs."

"I already told you, babe, I'm not letting that happen."

Piper looked up and studied Xavier's golden brown eyes, less amber than the day before. They practically glowed against his dark skin and he looked amazingly gorgeous with thick arms and a broad chest in that tight shirt. "I believe you."

Xavier was still a bit of a mystery to her, but she knew he liked to be in control. He challenged Caleb whenever he could, but usually they were a united front. There wasn't a lot they disagreed on when it came to her.

Out of the three of them Xavier was the most superstitious and wary of any of the other paranormals. He really disliked demons and witches and so had refused to meet with Jess. Niko was the only one out of them willing to touch witch magic so he had to stay with her to use it.

Caleb couldn't care less about the other paranormals, not really. He didn't like that he couldn't trust demons, but overall they didn't bother him in the same way they did Xavier.

"What aren't you telling me?" she finally asked him. "Why aren't you happy in Crescent City?"

Xavier's eyes widened in surprise. "What makes you think I'm not?"

She shrugged and opened the next demon book which was in Sanskrit. "You don't talk about it, and when it's brought up you change the subject or redirect to Niko."

He took her hand in his and sighed. "I didn't want to join the Army, but after serving, I wasn't ready to leave when Caleb ordered it. I liked being overseas. The desert feels right to me. Not all those fucking trees and rain. My leopard was happy over there. Caleb felt it too, but he was Alpha. He had to go back and retake the pride from his Third before chaos erupted."

EMMA DEAN

Xavier shook his head. "We were deployed usually for a year or so at a time and not much out of the ordinary happened while we were gone. We could have stayed for another tour, but the pride was getting antsy. The crocs were quiet for a while. Then they decided to move on us a few years ago and tried to murder the leopards in Tahoe. We only managed to save the kitten, Charlotte."

Piper squeezed his hand, but didn't say anything.

Xavier shrugged. "I felt free from all the bullshit for the first time in my life while we were overseas. When we came back I still didn't have any discernable skills or money so I learned how to weld and now I do that, but it's not the same. When we were in the Army we had a purpose, and we got to see the world."

Piper chewed on her lip and looked down at the first page of the demon book. "Well, you can still travel. Would you like to come to Egypt with me sometime? I have to go back at least once to finish my thesis."

He grinned at her and kissed her gently. "I'd love something like that. Does that mean you're warming up to the idea of staying with us?"

She was honestly surprised no one had asked her already. Caleb had been so careful to only answer her questions. It was easy to see he was terrified she would run away. But the reason she'd asked those questions was because of the opposite.

As more time passed with them the more the bond between them all strengthened. Piper could feel it deep in her chest. Every time she thought of them her heart leapt. They turned her on in ways she'd never thought she'd experience again after her ex, and then managed to top him.

What she'd been trying to come to terms with this whole time was the idea that there were three of them and only one

144

of her. Not only that – the intense emotions she already felt, and they only built every time one of her leopards did something sweet or nice. Like when Xavier had brought her breakfast in bed, and obviously waited for her to finish with Niko?

Her apartment wasn't that big and she hadn't been quiet.

No, what she'd never considered before was three men that were one hundred percent completely hers, no sharing required. But they didn't care that they all shared her. Piper had always had fantasies of sleeping with two men at once, and of course had been curious about the double penetration.

But it never crossed her mind to think she could have that always, or heck, add a third on top of *that*. Why not though... because it was unconventional? Piper had never been the conventional type, and she supposed this was just further proof.

She'd already decided she wanted to go to Crescent City with them, but only after Caleb had told her everything she'd needed to know. Now...she wasn't sure how to talk to her dad about it or finish her doctorate. Piper refused to give either of those two things up and she was having a hard time figuring out the logistics.

"I want to stay with you," she said slowly. Piper tilted her head at Xavier. "It's hard to say because I haven't known you for very long, but I have strong feelings for all three of you. The idea of letting you leave at the end of the two weeks physically hurts and makes me sad. I don't want to be alone again – just me and Cat Solo, even if he is good company."

Xavier took her face gently in his hands and kissed her long and slow. "I love you, Piper."

Hearing him say it electrified her. "Do you really?" she asked. "But how can you be sure?"

He shrugged, reached down and pulled her chair closer.

"I've never felt this way about anyone before in my life. I can feel the way our souls are connected, feel what you feel, and all I want is to live every day with you – learning more about you. I hope there will always be something new."

She nodded slowly. "That's how I feel."

He tapped her nose and chuckled. "Then why do you still sound unsure?"

It was difficult to explain, but Piper had never really liked big change. She didn't trust emotions really as they were unpredictable. It didn't help that she'd lived in Sacramento her whole life. "Well, I won't leave my dad so he needs to come too, and Caleb already said he could join the pride. But really...it's this place. It's this library and the Hellenic Collection and my doctorate. I refuse to leave it incomplete."

Xavier stood and pulled her out of her chair. He barely flexed his arms and she was lifted off her feet. Instinctually she wrapped her legs around his waist and her arms around his neck. "Someone could see," she hissed.

"No one is currently in the library," Xavier whispered, carrying her into one of the study rooms. "I have shifter hearing, remember?" He set her down on the table and closed the door, and then peeled his shirt off to cover the window.

"What are you doing?" she squeaked.

Xavier didn't answer her question. Instead he undid his belt. "We have libraries in Crescent City," he told her instead. He stepped closer and yanked her against him, hiking up her skirt. "And if you need me to drive you here two or three times a week to finish your doctorate I will."

He pulled her panties to the side and rubbed his thumb over her clit and then slid a finger inside. "God, you're already wet for me."

Piper gasped at the sensation, but she stared up at him in

complete disbelief. "You would really drive six hours there and then back three times a week for me?"

Xavier removed his hand and replaced it with his cock, yanking her onto him. She moaned and threw her head back as he completely filled her. "I would do it every single day if you asked."

Then he grabbed her ass and lifted her up. Piper held onto his shoulders tight and stared into his eyes. "Because you love me?"

"Because I love you," he murmured against her lips and then he thrust into her.

Piper would have thought she'd be tired from all the sex, but it was like her libido was in overdrive. She couldn't get enough of them, and each one was so different. Xavier was rough and sweet, letting her ride him as he took all her weight.

He went so deep she could feel the orgasm build already. She breathed heavily as she held on, her forehead pressed against his as she stared into his eyes and they glowed a vibrant gold she'd seen only once before – right before Caleb had shifted.

"I've never had sex in my library before," she told him, keeping the pace slow and steady, putting off her orgasm.

"Finally I'm fucking first at something," Xavier said, turning so he could press her up against the wall.

She gasped and rode him hard until she couldn't hold back any more. Piper bit down on his shoulder to keep from screaming as she came. Xavier groaned against her neck as he came with her. It made the sensation a thousand times more intense and she dug her nails into his back – Piper refused to be that obnoxious couple.

"I'm pretty sure you were the first one to kiss me," she teased when she could catch her breath.

He laughed at that. "So, you with us, babe?" Xavier kissed

her neck and then pulled back to look into her eyes. His thumb caressed her face and she smiled at him.

"I'm with you."

He kissed her hard and rough, sliding his tongue into her mouth and taking over her body as he rubbed against her so aftershocks rippled over her. "Good, because I'm pretty sure the three of us would die without you."

Piper slid down and laughed, grabbing a few Kleenexes from the box. "You can be so dramatic."

Xavier chuckled as he buckled his pants back up and then he froze. It was exactly like watching Cat Solo react to a noise he didn't recognize. Xavier even tilted his head to listen. "Someone's here," he whispered, grabbing his shirt from the window.

Piper felt adrenaline and fear flood her veins and her heart clenched. Xavier grabbed her hand and pulled her down to the floor when she froze. He slid his phone out of his pocket and she watched as he sent a group text to Niko and Caleb.

"We'll have backup soon, but we need to get out of here."

"The witch library is closer," she told him. "And I bet it's spelled."

Xavier put on his shirt and then studied her. "Do you remember how to open the door?"

She was too scared to say another word so Piper nodded.

This wasn't like when the three of them had come into her library to look for her. This was a real threat. If Xavier was worried, then she should be too. Did this have something to do with the curse or was this something else entirely?

Piper wasn't sure which would be worse.

"All right, follow my lead, stick close, and do everything I tell you," Xavier told her, his hand on the doorknob. "Promise me you will do everything I say without question or hesitation." His golden brown eyes searched hers desperately.

She nodded, knowing it could mean life or death if she didn't. "I'm with you."

He kissed her one last time and then opened the door. Piper prayed they were just overreacting. Then she took Xavier's hand and followed him out into the library stacks, crossing her fingers that whatever was out there, wasn't there to harm them. But even she knew how ridiculously naïve that sounded.

CHAPTER FIFTEEN

XAVIER

Xavier had been in plenty of high stress situations in the Army and overseas. He'd dealt with civilians in combat areas, but he'd never had his mate with him in a potentially dangerous environment. It changed the entire game.

He mentally cursed himself for not insisting she take a vacation when they first got there. If she'd been at the apartment this wouldn't even be an issue right now. But no, fucking Caleb had to insist on some level of normalcy while she adjusted to them.

Her clammy hand in his had him on high alert. This wasn't just any situation. The scent on the air – standing water and fish – told him it was crocs in the library, fucking crocs.

Piper's heartbeat was loud enough he knew the crocs could hear it too. There was no chance in hell they'd get out of the library or even to the underground one before they found them. He hoped Niko would be there soon.

"I can smell you, feline," a gravelly voice whispered.

Xavier gritted his teeth and darted from one stack to the other, pulling Piper along with him. From the footsteps it sounded like there were at least two of the crocs, but probably three. Thank fuck Piper couldn't hear them or this would have been a thousand times more difficult. She was already on the edge of panic.

They moved again and she snagged a book off the shelf.

He almost laughed. Almost.

"Your defenseless human isn't smart enough to get out of this."

Fuck, there were four of them. Xavier did the math and ground his teeth together. Unless Piper could take care of at least one there was a good chance he would be overwhelmed. Niko better hurry the fuck up.

"There you are," a man said, popping out from behind one of the stacks of books. His teeth were nasty and a few were missing. Then he reached out for Piper.

Piper didn't just throw the book. She held it with both hands and swung it like a bat. The croc went down like a rock and then she fucking pulled Xavier along. "Pretty much the only thing War and Peace is good for," she whispered.

Xavier couldn't hide his smile as they gave up trying to be sneaky and ran for the witch library.

Then two more crocs jumped out and blocked their path. Without hesitation Xavier put his body between them and Piper. Where the *fuck* was Niko?

"Just hand her over, feline, and we won't hurt you."

Xavier snarled and then whipped around when the hair on the back of his neck raised in warning. He kept Piper behind him with one arm around her. There were three crocs now and one pointed a gun at him. The other two were armed with knives, but thankfully not guns.

They wanted her alive.

A rumbling growl filled the space and suddenly Niko leapt in his leopard form, teeth clamping down on the outstretched arm. The croc screamed and the tangy smell of blood was all Xavier could smell before the sound of bones cracking resonated through them all.

He had to give Piper credit, she didn't scream or cower. She just held onto him tight and watched Niko ravage the fuck out of the croc, tearing him to pieces.

Xavier focused his attention on the other two. "Piper I need you to run as fast as you can to the fountain outside. Caleb should be here as soon as he can. Call your dad... whatever you need to do, just get out of here."

Her grip tightened. "I'm not leaving you and Niko."

There was no point arguing. She was stubborn as fuck so he released her and stepped forward. "Let's go," he told the crocs. "I dare you to take her from me."

Both of them attacked at the same time and Xavier pushed Piper farther behind him. He could fight just as good in his human form as he could in his leopard form. He dodged a punch, caught the wrist and twisted so the arm was over his shoulder and his back to the croc.

The other punched him in the gut, but Xavier tensed and sucked it up while he yanked down hard on the other's arm. The crack and scream that followed added to the racket. They'd catch the attention of someone soon and Xavier gritted his teeth. Clean up would be brutal.

Where was a witch when you needed one? The irony of the thought didn't escape him.

The croc in front of him went to attack again and Xavier kicked straight into his chest. He flew back into a shelf. Then Xavier flipped the other over and onto his back. Without hesitating he slid the knife from his boot and sank it into the croc's throat.

Before he could move the other screeched. Xavier looked up and saw Piper tazing the shit out of the one she'd knocked out as he tried to come after Xavier and Niko again.

Fuck she was perfect. But also vulnerable. He got up and moved. But before he could reach her the second croc grabbed him.

He had never heard anything as terrifying as Piper's scream and the smell of fresh human blood. Xavier partially shifted and ignored the excruciating pain. He ripped through the tender skin of the second croc's throat. He had to get back to her, but Niko was already there, jumping onto the back of the one attacking her.

Then Xavier was at her side and checking her over. Her face was too pale and her eyes unfocused. "Piper," he murmured, looking for the wound. When she didn't respond he raised his voice. "Piper! Are you with me?"

Her arm had a long slice from the elbow to the wrist. Xavier cursed and ripped his shirt off. This needed stitches as soon as possible or she could bleed out. Panic rose up to choke him and he hoped to God Caleb would be there soon.

"Keep that one alive for questioning," he snarled at Niko.

The leopard growled his displeasure, but he did as he was told. Caleb would be there soon and he would need answers. "Shift back and call a cleaning team. Piper is hurt."

Instantly Niko was human and naked. "Give me your phone, all my stuff is outside."

He handed it over without question and then tightened his shirt over the wound. "You okay, babe? How are you feeling?"

"They're dead," she whispered.

Xavier followed her line of sight and cursed when he saw

all the blood. "Yes, they are. If we hadn't killed them the Mayacamas Mountain Wolf Pack would have. Sacramento is their territory. We did them a favor. Now look at me."

Finally she did and her forehead had beads of sweat. Xavier frowned and gently placed the back of his hand against her skin. He didn't like how clammy she was. There was a lot of blood and she'd had a shock. It was highly possible she'd never seen a dead body before.

Xavier cursed internally. He knew how to deal with all of this shit. How many times had he told civilians everything was going to be all right? How many times had he stayed with the ones that wouldn't be?

"We should take her to the hospital," Niko said, hanging up. "The wolves are sending their cleaners for the bodies. Then the witches are sending a team to cleanse the library of any traces of blood and psychic energy and to wipe any surveillance or memories."

Xavier wrapped Piper up in his arms and held her close, trying to ease some of her pain with contact alone. "Call Caleb and ask him what to do."

"Caleb is already here," their Alpha snarled.

He didn't even look twice at the bodies. Caleb went straight for Piper and removed the shirt covering her wound. He hissed in a breath and then scooped her up in his arms. Piper didn't even protest which in itself was a very bad sign. "I'm taking her to the hospital. Stay here and deal with this. Question that fucker over there and then get rid of him."

Piper was in competent hands and Caleb would keep her safe. He turned to the one Niko had dealt with. Both legs were broken and the croc wasn't going anywhere.

Xavier grinned, relieved to have a direction. "With pleasure."

He studied the croc for a moment as they waited for

Caleb to leave. Once the sound of the door closing reached his ears he cocked his head in question. "What did you think you were going to accomplish here?" Xavier asked.

Niko's naked ass disappeared when Xavier focused on the croc. The dumb fucker just laughed even though he knew there was no way out of this for him.

"Why would I tell you, feline?"

Niko came back fully dressed and with an extra shirt he tossed Xavier. "Maybe we'll spare your life."

"Your kind would never spare a croc," the other shifter spat. "Why would you when two hundred years ago you killed all our young?"

Xavier rolled his eyes. "I'm sick and tired of hearing this bullshit story. We moved out of your territory a hundred and fifty years ago. We don't know what started the blood feud. But still, y'all won't leave us the fuck alone about it so now we're here and you have two broken legs instead of enjoying the muggy heat of Miami. Could you please explain why before I just remove your legs?"

Niko set one of their duffels on a nearby table and Xavier crouched down so he was eye level with the croc. "You know, I've heard the same story. That a whole generation of kittens were slaughtered by crocodiles and so we murdered an entire pack of crocs in return. Y'all just need to let it go."

The croc growled when Niko tossed him one of the longer knives and Xavier caught it without having to look. They'd done this a thousand times before, but he knew this time wouldn't be any different. The answers never changed.

"The demon tried to kill our witch so we came to retrieve the girl ourselves," the croc rumbled. God, they could be so damn ugly. "We don't need the girl. Just her blood." A rasping laugh filled the room and Xavier gritted his teeth, barely holding on to his patience. "Guess we should have thought about that when we made the contract."

"Guess you should have," Xavier told him, and then thrust the knife into the croc's heart and twisted. He died almost instantly and good riddance.

If they didn't hide in the swamps and shit Xavier would have killed every last one of them. But it was suicide to go after them in their own territory and they were sneaky bastards usually. "Take pictures of everything before the wipe. We need to show the Council proof, that our allegations aren't just part of the blood feud."

Niko was already on it, taking pictures of the other three. He nodded and then jerked his head up and sniffed. It was difficult to smell much with so much coppery blood filling the air, but there was a slight sound.

Xavier grabbed one of the guns from the duffel and flipped the safety off.

A scrawny kid walked into the library with a backpack slung over his shoulder and then froze when he saw the rifle pointed at his face and the bodies everywhere. He laughed awkwardly and held up his hands while the blood drained from his face. "This isn't where I parked my car." Then he nervously turned to leave.

He was about to move when a pretty girl with blonde hair walked up to the kid with this big, reassuring smile. Then she reached up and placed her entire hand over his face. Instantly the kid went limp and crumbled to the ground. Xavier gritted his teeth when he realized she wasn't just a girl, she was a fucking witch.

She looked down at the kid and then up at Niko. "Seems you've been having some trouble."

Xavier would recognize that sleepy, husky voice anywhere. "What are you doing here, Morgan?"

She glanced at him and then stepped over the kid, tucking a stray piece of hair behind her ear. Her ponytail swung behind her and she went to give Niko a hug. "Saving your ass apparently, show some gratitude X."

"My name's Xavier to you." He crossed his arms over his chest. Fucking witches.

Then there were five more and three wolves crawling all over everything. Xavier rolled his shoulders back in irritation and flipped the safety back on. He couldn't wait to take Piper and get the hell out of Sacramento. Crescent City wasn't the most hip and trendy city to live in, but at least it was his territory.

"Thanks for coming Morgan, but you didn't really have to," Niko told her, grabbing her arm and pulling her over to them. "I don't think there's much you can do."

She smiled up at him and adjusted the oversized grey sweater she had on over her black leather pants. The girl was a weirdo and looked barely eighteen. Then that blue-eyed gaze whipped to him and Xavier flinched. Fucking witches man.

"I'm here to see Piper, not deal with...this," she said, waving at the dead bodies. "If you guys mess this up with her..."

"We're not going to," Xavier snapped. "Now why come all the way down here to see her when you could have just called?"

"Do you know any witches with healing abilities?" she demanded, that husky voice sharp as nails for the first time ever.

"X, just let her help. She's one of the good ones."

Morgan smirked. "We're all supposed to be neutral. I'd say we're not good, or bad." She picked up one of the little witch balls she'd given Niko, inspected it, and then put it back. "Where is she?"

"She's at the hospital with Caleb," Xavier grumbled, watching the cleaners and the witches work. One of them even carried the sleeping kid outside. He craned his neck to see that they'd put him on one of the couches, just like any tired student between classes. "Is he going to remember anything?"

"Of course not," Morgan snorted.

She was quiet for a moment while she looked down at one of her rings and spun it on her finger over and over. Xavier didn't like witches, but this one was so different. She didn't lord what she could do over anyone's head. She just helped them. He could like her without having to like witches.

"Look, I've been doing a lot of scrying, and I've been reading the bones, tarot...pretty much anything short of blood magic," Morgan told them, keeping that strange voice quiet so she wouldn't be overheard. "If the crocs take Piper it will be the end of the Klamath Mountain Pride. Normally I wouldn't care. Shifter crap is none of my business unless the Council says otherwise, or a friend asks for my help." She nodded at Niko and then paused again, twirling that fucking ring around and around.

A feeling of dread settled in the pit of Xavier's stomach. Regardless of how he felt about the covens, he knew better than to ignore a warning from them, and this one...this one sounded like it could be very, very bad.

"If the Klamath Mountain Pride falls, then war will break out between the West Coast Pride and the Miami crocs," she told them. "This war would decimate both shifters, and tip the balance. Demons would get involved more than they already are, and hunters would be dispatched. The chaos will cause a lot of issues, but the main one is that Piper's blood is extremely powerful. It can be used to unlock one of the Seven Seals if the right spell is used."

Xavier froze as he took that in. "You mean one of the Seven Seals of Hell?"

She nodded and then glanced over her shoulder. "It's not quite what you think as Hell is just another plane of existence. But witches have used the Seven Seals to lock away some pretty awful things, including the apocalypse. Having her as your mate is unfortunate." She shrugged a shoulder and pulled her sleeves down over her hands. "You will have to protect her and her blood, and your children's blood for the rest of your lives."

Niko and Xavier shared a look. It was a lot to take in, but Piper was their mate.

"I fucking dare anyone to try and take her," Xavier said.

Morgan smiled then and crossed her arms over her chest like she was cold, but maybe she was just tired. Witches used up mad amounts of energy. "Can you take me to see her?"

Niko looked to Xavier for the answer to that question and he was pleased as shit to have been given the opportunity to say no. There was a reason Niko was his best friend, the crazy white boy.

"Yeah, you can see her, but don't bewitch her or anything like that."

Morgan gave him a secret smile. "I wouldn't dare try and bewitch your mate. I only do that to the single ladies."

He blinked and then glanced at Niko who just grinned at him. "She's not your average witch," he told him.

Xavier packed up their stuff and gave the cleaners and witches a nod of thanks. The bodies were nothing more than ash that was being vacuumed up and the blood was completely removed from the carpets. They did good work. "How did you even meet this one?" he asked Niko.

"She and my sister were friends before Morgan's parents moved to Portland. We stayed in touch. She came to Anastasia's funeral." Niko grabbed Piper's purse from her desk and the demon books as they passed.

Shit, he'd had no idea they were that close. "Have I met her before?"

"I think you did at the funeral, but you've never stuck around when a witch showed up and I get why. That one who told us our mate would curse us was a bitch."

Xavier shook his head and held the door open for Niko. "Well, she was right in a roundabout way."

Piper was the best thing to ever happen to him though. Morgan's warning didn't scare him. Xavier would fight for her for the rest of his life if he had to and die happy.

CHAPTER SIXTEEN

PIPER

The ride to the hospital was a blur. Somehow Caleb got her in right away with no wait time at all. It had to be the panicked Alpha voice and all the blood. She felt a bit woozy, but she just couldn't stop thinking about those dead crocs.

Piper knew what a blood feud was; she'd studied enough of them. Her patron goddess was the goddess of justice and execution in Ancient Egypt after all. She wasn't unused to the idea of death as Egyptians were all about it, but seeing it in real life was a whole other thing.

She knew her father had shot people before – criminals. And were the crocs any different? They'd tried to take her, or kill her...it wasn't really clear, but she'd guess that her blood was more important than she was.

Xavier and Niko had killed those people though...for her. Part of her was horrified and the other part was insanely grateful. There wasn't anything these three wouldn't do for her. They were willing to risk their lives for love, just like Marc Antony did for Cleopatra.

"How are you feeling?" the doctor asked when she walked in, reading the chart. Then she took one look at Caleb and didn't waste any time with pleasantries.

A nurse was called in and suddenly someone was placing an I.V. into Piper's arm while the doctor cleaned the blood off her other arm. The cut was deep and it went from her wrist to inside her elbow, the entire length of her forearm, Piper was covered in blood and it hadn't stopped yet. "Was this self-harm?" the doctor asked.

Piper shook her head, knowing anything Caleb said would be disregarded. "It was an accident. I was cutting a watermelon with a new, very sharp knife and slipped." Thankfully the large slice looked like someone had slipped or it would have been more difficult to tell a convincing lie.

Caleb refused to let go of her hand and was generally in the way while everyone worked on her. The panic in his eyes, the fear he felt – she could feel it too. Piper didn't once look away from him while the doctor gave the nurse orders and then started stitching her up. She ordered a blood transfusion when Piper started to feel faint from all the blood loss.

Caleb was quietly losing his mind – she could see it. He needed her to be okay. "I'm going to be all right," she told him. "It's just a scratch."

"I should have been there," he whispered.

Piper squeezed his hand. "You can't be everywhere."

Then the doctor was giving them care instructions and Piper felt sleepy. They must have given her drugs. She just needed to rest her eyes.

When she opened them again the room was empty except for Caleb, the lights were off, and the beeping of the monitors was quiet. He was resting his head on her bed with his arm wrapped around her stomach, playing a game on his phone. "Hey," she whispered, reaching out to stroke his hair back. Piper tried to get a look at what he was playing, but he turned it off the second she moved.

Caleb looked up and searched her face for a long time. His hands were shaking when he reached for her, and she could have sworn there were tears in his eyes.

"I'm going to be okay," she reassured him. "It's just a flesh wound." The joke fell flat though when Caleb practically curled into himself to rest his head on her hand.

"When I got that text," he said quietly. "I was terrified you'd be dead before I could get there."

"But I'm not." This big, burly man was practically crying because she'd gotten hurt. "Look Caleb, I'm not dead. You didn't fail, and I know you won't. Now come sit with me."

She scooted over to make room for him, and she knew just how wrecked he was because he crawled into the tiny hospital bed without question, careful of her injury, and then wrapped his arms around her. Piper rested her head on his chest and sighed contentedly.

"I've always been too late," he whispered into her hair. "If something happened to you...I'd probably go feral."

"What does that mean?" she asked, afraid of the answer.

"Turn into a leopard and never turn back. Run wild in the wilderness until I die."

Piper shuddered and snuggled into Caleb's hard body. He held her close and rubbed his chin across the top of her hair, the bristles of his beard comforting. Somehow he was always so careful with her despite how big and strong he was. "That sounds awful," she whispered.

"It would be better than living without you."

EMMA DEAN

Those words broke her heart and made her fall for him even harder. Piper turned in his arms and looked up at him. "I want you to turn me into a cat shifter."

Caleb looked down at her in utter shock for a long time. The only sound was the monitors beeping and the noise of the hospital outside the door.

"What did you say?" he finally asked.

"I want to be a cat shifter, like you. And I want to move to Crescent City after this is all over. Because I love you." Piper smiled up at him and almost laughed at the disbelief on his face. If she didn't know how hard this whole mate thing had been for him she might have been offended.

The air whooshed out of him like it had been knocked from his chest. "Well, we can make the arrangements for the claiming ceremony." Caleb sounded like he almost didn't believe what he was saying.

Piper kissed him and his hands immediately dove into her hair. He kissed her like a dying man – as if this would be the last time he'd be able to communicate everything he was feeling into one action.

"I love you too, Piper," he finally said. She knew how hard it was for him to admit such a thing out loud with real words, but she adored him for it.

She was overwhelmed by his feelings, by his love. But she was also wrapped up in them like they were a blanket and it warmed her soul. It took away her pain and Piper felt settled inside. She knew this was the right path for her – Caleb was right for her despite their rough beginning. He was hers, as were Xavier and Niko.

There was a knock at the door and Caleb growled in annoyance.

Piper laughed and told them to come in. She thought it

166

would be just another nurse, or maybe Niko and Xavier, but it was a small blonde woman who smiled at her like she'd just woken up. It was oddly erotic.

"I said no bewitching Morgan!" Xavier complained from the hall.

Piper blinked in surprise when he and Niko came barreling in after the witch. So this was the infamous Morgan. "I'm sorry, what?" she asked.

"Don't mind him," Morgan said gently. "He's still coming to terms with the fact that he doesn't hate me."

Piper laughed. Then Xavier and Niko were by her side, looking her over, asking her a million questions. "I'm fine," she told them. "All stitched up and they're running tests while the blood transfusion finishes."

"Tell them you don't need any more tests and you're ready to be discharged," Morgan said in that quiet, warm voice that had a surprising amount of steel hidden in it. "I'll heal you the second we're out of here."

"You can do that? I didn't know witches could heal." Piper watched as the girl came over and took her hand, eyes staring off into the distance at nothing. Morgan looked like she was barely out of high school. "How old are you?"

"Twenty-four, now shh. I need to make sure you're healthy." Then Morgan closed her eyes and Piper could feel something searching inside of her. It was warm and pleasant and gentle, but it still creeped her out.

"No poison in your blood and it looks like they replaced what you lost without issue. Nothing else hiding in there. Aside from the cut and the drugs they gave you, you're perfectly healthy. The sooner we leave the better since we can't protect you in public places like we can in a house. Though the Pride's estate would be better as it's already got a mess of protections rooted into the land and the foundations," Morgan muttered.

"I'm not leaving Sacramento without talking to my dad," Piper said firmly.

Morgan blinked and slowly came back to them. Then she took a step back and released Piper. "Of course not. Your father will agree to move so don't stress about that."

This girl...was strange. Piper didn't want to simply believe her. It went against everything she knew, everything she was taught. How could one person hold so much power – how could they know so much?

Then a nurse came into the room with papers for Piper. It wasn't much work to convince the nurse to release her. Per the time and date on her discharge papers, they'd only been at the hospital for a few hours. But getting all three of her leopards out of there? They were so busy fighting for the room to fuss over her she was getting suffocated.

"Enough," she snapped. "No one touch me until we get to my apartment. I'm fully capable of walking on my own."

All three of them grumbled but did as she asked, opening doors when they could and generally herding her from all angles. Morgan just wrapped her arms around herself with a smile and stayed close.

Once they were all loaded into the truck Morgan took her injured arm and muttered under her breath in a language that was familiar yet not.

It was like being submerged in a warm bath. All the aches and pains in her body disappeared and she felt completely relaxed. There was no remaining wooziness from the painkillers or any of the burning sensation from her arm.

Morgan sat back when she was finished, looking even more tired than she normally did. "I'll have Jess pick me up at your apartment if that's okay. I just wanted to meet you Piper and do what I could to help."

Piper unraveled the bandages, almost scared to look, but her skin was whole. There was only a white line to show what had happened. Morgan had even removed the stitches from her body. It took her a few seconds to really register what she was seeing. Piper had to touch her skin and even then she hardly believed it.

"Thank you." Piper threw her arms around Morgan and gave her a bear hug. Even the witch-leery shifters murmured their thanks.

"Let's get you home so I can feed you, and you also need to call your dad," Xavier told her.

Piper thanked Morgan again and took her purse from Xavier as Caleb pulled out of the hospital's parking lot. When she took out her phone Morgan snagged it from her. Piper watched as the witch took out a little stick attached to a long necklace and then drew onto the back of her phone. A few words in Latin and she handed it back.

"A parting gift, Piper Kostopoulos. You'll never have to charge your phone again." Morgan closed her eyes after tucking the necklace with the stick and various other charms back under her sweater. It looked like she'd actually fallen asleep after a few minutes.

"Man, I could totally use that parting gift," Niko muttered.

"It's mine," Piper teased. "Sorry, I'm not giving it to you."

These people...they'd all barreled into her life, shoving into it and demanding room and her attention...Piper had hated it at first, but now it just felt right. Morgan had come all the way down from Portland just to make sure she was all right. Jess from Los Angeles, and then there was Eisheth.

How was she supposed to want normal ever again?

Piper supposed she didn't have to as she looked at the suddenly full battery symbol on her phone. Tech magic...for a brief moment Piper wished she was a witch, but the responsibility seemed too much for her. She wanted to enjoy her mates and her life once they figured all this other stuff out.

She tapped her father's contact, not looking forward to this conversation.

"Piper, is everything okay sweetie?"

"Dad, do you have time to come by my apartment tonight?"

The silence on the other end made her stomach flip-flop with nerves.

"Are you hurt?" he demanded.

"No, Dad, but I was. There was an incident earlier today at the library. Don't worry, a witch, um...healed me." Piper winced, knowing how ridiculous that sounded, especially to someone like her dad. "Could you come over? There's something I want to ask you."

"If it's about working anymore the answer is definitely not. You aren't going back there until this madness is over."

Xavier and Caleb shared a look in the front of the truck's cab.

"Dad!" Piper winced again and glanced at Morgan, but the witch was completely out. "Just come over to my stupid apartment!"

"Fine. I'll be there in ten minutes."

She hung up the phone and sighed. Why was her father so fracking difficult sometimes?

"We don't have to do this now," Caleb said quietly.

"No," she snapped, realizing just how tired she was by the sound of her voice. "I want to set these plans in place. If the Pride's property is really that much safer, we should go there. And I want to be a shifter so I can be faster and stronger – to protect myself instead of always being the damsel in distress."

Xavier looked surprised about the shifter part, but he nodded. "Although I just want you to know babe, you're not really a damsel in distress. You knocked that croc out with a fucking book and then tased the shit out of him."

Caleb chuckled at that. "Man, I wish I could have seen that."

Niko tentatively put an arm around her shoulders and Piper leaned into him. They managed to turn her bad moods around, and that was pretty impressive. Usually no one was able to get rid of her attitude except Patrick, and only because he was her dance partner.

There was a pang in her chest at the idea of leaving him, their partnership, and their competitions. How would she break the bad news to him? They'd worked together for a long time, but not only that, he'd been the closest thing to a friend she'd had before Caleb, Niko, and Xavier had introduced her to a whole new, paranormal world.

Caleb parked outside her apartment building and she sighed. It was completely dark and only the streetlights gave her any ability to see anything. If she moved, she'd never have her own space again, but did she really want it now that she knew what it was like to be surrounded by so much love and care?

It wasn't like they suffocated her either. All three of them were quiet when she read and sometimes Niko read over her shoulder, but generally they did their own thing, and in her tiny apartment with all four of them and her cat, it was no small thing for her not to feel claustrophobic with them constantly around.

"What's wrong?" Niko asked softly.

The other two turned to look at her in concern as well.

Piper shrugged sheepishly. "I know I said I'm ready for this next step, but then I thought about Patrick and our upcoming competitions..." she trailed off and looked down at the thin white scar along her entire forearm, all that was left of her physical trauma. "I don't want to give that up."

"You don't have to," Caleb told her, twisting so he could grab her hand and squeeze. "You can still compete with him this season, but after that you'll compete with me."

Her mouth dropped open in shock, but then a slow smile took over her face. "Really?" she asked in disbelief. "That's something you want to do?" That kind of partnership would be a dream.

Caleb smiled and both Niko and Xavier looked shocked at the transformation in their Alpha. He really did look like a god when he smiled. "We can even try for pro competitions if you want. I will always make time for you Piper, even if I am Alpha."

"I would love that."

Niko opened the door and offered her his hand. Piper took it and then looked up when she heard a loud motorcycle pull up. She watched as the rider stopped next to the truck and then put the kickstand down, but left the engine running. They flipped up their visor and somehow Piper wasn't surprised to find Jess winking at her.

Her leopards let Jess open the other door and catch Morgan before she fell out.

"Is she going to be all right?" Piper asked.

Morgan got her bearings and then took a little pill out of her pocket and popped it in her mouth. She waved to Piper through the open doors of the truck and instantly she looked more awake. Morgan took the spare helmet from Jess and then climbed on the back of the motorcycle like she'd done it a thousand times before.

"Her girlfriend back in Portland has a motorcycle too," Niko whispered in her ear. "She just took a caffeine pill with a bit of magic in it, she'll be fine."

Jess waved goodbye and then blew a kiss to the cop car pulling up before she peeled out of the little cul-de-sac.

Her father got out of the car with a frown. "If I wasn't off duty," he mumbled.

Piper couldn't help but laugh at that. Somehow she doubted he would have ever caught Jess.

"What did you need me here for, Piper?" her dad asked, adjusting the belt of his uniform. Then he grabbed her hand and studied the white line on her arm. "This is a new scar."

"Let's go upstairs and I'll explain everything."

Her dad sighed but nodded. "Are you going to be cooking Xavier?" he asked, falling in step with him. "I know it's late, but it's dinner for us around this time."

X smiled and chatted with her dad about what he planned to make this time and Piper watched the two of them walk into her apartment complex. She realized then that Morgan was probably right. Her dad wouldn't have any issues with this move. What was it about these three that set him so at ease?

Piper shook her head. She wasn't going to complain or question it.

"Let me carry this," Caleb said, taking her purse from her. "You and Niko go ahead of me. I'll make sure it's safe."

She did as she was told and walked slowly into the complex and up the stairs. The sound of the crickets was all that filled the silence so late at night. Piper didn't even know what time it was, but it had to be after midnight and she felt exhausted.

The library, her favorite place, was no longer safe. Four crocodile shifters had died there. She didn't want to ask what had happened to the bodies either. Though if she were going to become a cat shifter she supposed she'd become far more intimate with these kinds of situations.

"So this claiming ceremony," she said, pausing outside her door so her dad didn't overhear. "Is it time specific, like only on a full moon?"

Caleb shook his head and kissed her cheek. "Nope, anytime, anywhere."

"And will I turn into a leopard, or some other kind of cat?"

Niko went inside and left her with Caleb, kissing her cheek too as he went by. The sound of Cat Solo attacking his legs and the curses that followed made her smile. For whatever reason her cat liked to lay in wait for Niko, but not the others.

Caleb smiled too and tucked a piece of hair behind her ear. "A leopard, babe. The specific type of shifter that turns you is what you end up as. That magic helps us keep track of any new shifters."

"What if Cat Solo hates me after?" The thought hadn't occurred to her until just now.

"He won't." Caleb wrapped his arms around her and squeezed. "Now let's go talk to your dad. I want to take you back to my territory as quickly as possible."

She nodded. "Okay, let's do this." Piper was more nervous than she probably should be. Her dad had always been supportive of her.

Piper stepped through her front door and then instantly froze. Niko and Xavier were laughing with her father in the kitchen, talking about the last football game while Xavier set up ingredients for dinner and Niko poured them all wine.

It was the strangest thing she'd ever seen, but it also made her warm inside. They were already like a family in a way and she crossed her fingers behind her back, hoping her dad wouldn't make this difficult.

"Dad," she said, stepping into the kitchen and taking a deep breath. "I want to move to Crescent City with them."

Her dad looked up and nodded, sipping his wine. "I figured as much."

"But I don't want to go without you," she told him.

At that Richard Kostopoulos paused and set down his glass of wine. "You want me to move to Crescent City with you? And do what, live where?"

Her heart clenched in fear and she looked to Caleb for help.

"Sir, you would be welcome in our pride as a human, all you'd have to do is register. I have some pull with the city, but I know they always need good cops – one who knows about the paranormal world would be invaluable since there are so many of us there." Caleb shrugged and put his arm around Piper's shoulders. "I could help you buy a house, or you could live at the Pride's estate with us. It's really up to you."

Her dad cocked his head to the side ever so slightly, and she saw the guys share a look – yes that's who she'd gotten that particular quirk from. "Well, if that's what you want Piper. I don't know what I'd do here by myself except get into trouble."

Piper laughed at that and went to hug her father. She was so lucky to have a dad like him. Tears ran down her cheeks as relief flooded her. He was one of the most important people in her life and she didn't know what she would do without him. "Thank you," she whispered when he hugged her back. "Thank you so much, Dad."

He kissed her cheek and she ignored the red on his cheeks and the tears in his eyes as he chucked her under the chin. "Someone's gotta keep an eye on these boys, make sure they treat you how you deserve to be treated – like the queen you are."

Caleb wrapped his arms around her waist and pulled her against his chest. "She'll be the queen of the pride," he said.

Piper couldn't stop smiling as she watched her dad go right back to discussing the football game with Niko and Xavier. This was exactly how she wanted the rest of her life to be.

CHAPTER SEVENTEEN

PIPER

After some really good spaghetti, meatballs, and garlic bread Piper had been sent to bed with orders to get some rest. It was silly really since Morgan had healed her, but she'd been so tired she was asleep before her head hit the pillow.

No one had crawled into her bed during the night and Piper was surprised to find she felt disappointed by that. It was strange how quickly things changed. Just a few weeks ago she'd been supremely content with her quiet little lifestyle, plugging away on her research, and only going out a few times a week for practice.

Now she couldn't imagine how she would live without the three of them. Piper enjoyed the one on one time she got with them, but she adored when they were all together, doing something like when they'd binged all the Star Wars movies and shows.

Piper smelled coffee. She grabbed her robe and wrapped

it around her pajama shorts and top. It was strange to have what felt like an infinite amount of time off. She'd accrued so much it wouldn't affect her pay. Normally the university had to beg her to go.

What would she do with so much free time?

She sighed and opened her door to find all three of them waiting for her. Piper jumped and then smacked all three of them on the arms. "You scared me! What are you guys doing standing outside my door like a bunch of creeps?"

"We heard you get up," Xavier explained.

"And we got you something," Niko said.

She looked at all three of them and then suddenly felt nervous. "What is it?" she demanded. "What did you do?"

Caleb just grinned and that scared her even more. "Well, we knew you would have a hard time enjoying your days off and we can't leave for Crescent City until I turn in everything to the Council and speak to them."

Piper gave him a look and went to go to the kitchen, but Niko stopped her. "It was Xavier's idea and it's really quite brilliant. A great way to waste some time."

"You didn't buy a game console did you? I really don't like video games." Piper crossed her arms over her chest and glared. She really just wanted some coffee.

"Even better. I had to really search, but when I found it Caleb went off and got it before you woke up," Xavier said. Then he stepped aside and right there on her coffee table was the biggest box of Legos she'd ever seen.

"Shut the front door!" Piper couldn't believe it. "Do you know how hard those are to find? Do you know how much they cost?!" She went straight to the box and inspected its sleek surface. It was brand spanking new, never been opened.

"Yeah, and apparently it takes like sixty hours to

complete," Xavier said with a grin. "But probably less if we all work on it."

"You guys bought me a freaking Millennium Falcon?" Piper heard her voice get a little screechy, but she didn't care. It was something she'd been meaning to buy since it came out, but they were always sold out. "How did you even find one?"

Piper couldn't bring herself to touch it. She wanted to enjoy it in its brand new state just a little while longer.

"Caleb and I called every store in the city, and even surrounding areas." Niko told her. "Xavier searched online, but we got lucky. One of the Lego stores had one so Caleb went right when they opened."

"We noticed all the boxes of Star Wars Legos you hide in the guest room closet," Caleb teased. "Why don't you display them?"

She blushed and ran a finger along the edge of the box. "It depends, but sometimes I like to build them again. Some people do puzzles. I do Legos. It helps me think when I get stuck on my thesis, or just need a mental break."

Then she wrapped one arm around Caleb, and the other around Xavier and Niko. "Thank you so much," she murmured, kissing each one on the cheek. "Are you sure you want to help me build it though?"

"Yes, of course," Xavier said. "You can put on that cartoon Star Wars show and we'll just hang out for the next few days while we wrap stuff up so we can leave."

"Even you Caleb?" she asked, feeling a bit flustered by their attention. "Surely you have important Alpha things to do."

He chuckled and slapped her ass. "Go get some coffee so we can start. I'll help when I'm not doing important Alpha things like ordering breakfast. Food is on the way."

Piper went into the kitchen with a massive smile on her face. "Oh man, my dad is going to be so jealous."

"We can invite him if you want," Niko said. "But I don't know his schedule."

She shrugged and watched the three of them working together. They seemed so much easier around each other than they did before. Whatever tension that was there was gone. Now they had a single-minded focus to work together and get things done.

However they'd operated in the pride before, Piper had a feeling they'd be intensely more efficient now.

"Yeah, let's see what my dad is doing later today, but I'd rather just enjoy the morning with the three of you alone," she said, pouring coconut creamer in her coffee and taking a sip. "It's been a while since I let myself just relax."

Niko came up and kissed her neck. "There are plenty of ways to relax."

She swatted him away with a laugh and went straight to the massive Lego box with her Millennium Falcon. "Maybe later, I want to open this now."

All three of them groaned but sat around the coffee table with her.

"Maybe we didn't think this through," Xavier teased. "Sex and *then* reveal the present that will take all day to complete."

"Come on, X. Piper is our mate, and you know this shit is just as much fun as the sex."

Xavier grumbled under his breath but he was smiling. Piper grinned as she sat on the couch and sipped her coffee. She was so ready for a little bit of normal with her mates – the chance for them all to get a little bit closer. Piper needed this right now.

"Don't touch," she said, smacking Xavier's hand from the

box. "I get to open it first."

Caleb and Niko laughed and then the doorbell rang. Caleb got up to get the food and Niko consoled Xavier.

It was going to be a good day.

Piper rolled over and checked the time on her phone. It was late, but she was still alone in her bed. Now would be as good a time as any.

She'd been confined to her apartment for two days. Piper wasn't allowed to leave, but Caleb or Niko left to replace the books she'd been reading on demons and shifters or to get food. They'd spent the entire first day talking and building her Falcon. Then she'd rewarded them with some pretty mind-blowing sex if she did say so herself. They'd definitely earned it.

Piper had learned a lot while they'd chatted and slowly built the Falcon, working as a team when they had to start putting the separate chunks together. She'd asked more about the paranormal world, but specifically shifters – leopard shifters to be exact.

The claiming ceremony had brought up a lot of questions. Like, if the leopards in the U.S. were dying out, why didn't they just turn humans into leopards like they were doing with her? Apparently there was a rule against that too. Anyone found making unsanctioned turns was brought before the Council. Usually the punishment was death.

Mates were allowed to be turned during a claiming ceremony, but any other had to be brought before the Council as a request. Accidents did happen. Feral shifters had and did bite humans randomly. Apparently an incident like that had happened up near Portland with a wolf pack and they'd had to put the shifter down.

Piper would never have guessed the paranormal world had just as much red tape and weird rules and laws as the human world did, although now that she thought about it she shouldn't have been surprised. They all shared this plane after all – or most of them did.

The second day Piper had studied as many of the demon and witch texts as she could. Of course if they thought she was working too hard they would distract her. The first time someone had gone down on her while she was reading had surprised her enough she'd dropped the book on their head. And demon texts weren't light.

It was what she imagined a honeymoon would be like. Endless sex, delicious food, and all the books she could want to read. But tomorrow they'd be going to Crescent City after Caleb finished turning in the rest of the proof and evidence he'd scrounged up to the Council.

Jessica had called and told Piper she'd been officially assigned their case now and would help in any way possible.

Piper quietly slipped out of her bed and then tip-toed to her door. She peered out and saw the three of them sleeping on the couch. After a long day she'd fallen asleep watching TV with them, and she guessed they'd put her to bed at some point. Knowing them they probably didn't want to disturb her so had watched something else...only to fall asleep together.

It was so adorable. The four of them had really bonded over the last two days. Niko was leaning into Caleb and Xavier had his feet on Niko's lap. It made her smile.

Then she turned and grabbed her boots and jacket. Piper went out to the balcony through the door from her bedroom feeling a little bad about not telling them, but...she needed to do this on her own. She was the only one who could bargain.

If she didn't know she'd be one hundred percent safe Piper would have told them. She stepped into her boots and didn't even close the door to her balcony, making sure the noise was at a minimum for sensitive cat ears. Thankfully the TV was still on, playing some animal documentary loud enough to cover up the small sounds.

Piper took out the piece of chalk from her back pocket and angled her phone so it reflected the moonlight on the surface like a mirror. She drew the pentagram and whispered Eisheth's true name. In less than a second he stood before her in a gorgeous linen suit, hands in his pockets and a shit-eating grin on his face.

"I knew you'd call me."

She put a finger to her lips and wiped her phone off before tucking it into her back pocket. Then she held out her hand for Eisheth and took off the talisman, slipping that into her pocket too. After all her reading she knew it had to be touching her skin to work. Eisheth's face grew serious and he nodded.

Then her lungs compressed and she couldn't breathe and everything hurt and then...there was light and sound and *air*. Piper let go of the demon and breathed deep. "Dang, I'm never going to get used to that."

Eisheth chuckled and put his hands back in his pockets. "There's this lovely little coffee shop around the corner that's open all night. Would you like to get a drink and tell me why you summoned me?"

Piper nodded and followed him down the dark alley towards the bright street. "Thanks for not killing me."

"I gave you my summoning name. The rules are a bit different," Eisheth said as he opened the door for her. "Start calling me for every little thing though and we might have issues."

She smiled and walked into the cozy little café. "If you just gave me your cell number we could chat like normal people."

Eisheth chuckled and followed her into the café that had a surprising number of people in it. The atmosphere was quiet though, the chatter a low murmur against chill music. Then a blonde waved from one of the booths and Piper recognized Jess instantly.

"I didn't realize we'd have company," she said as Eisheth directed her to the counter to order.

"Darling, I didn't invite her. Jess is a demon witch, remember? She does what she wants when she wants, and has the power, magic, and strength to back it up." Eisheth ordered three drinks, but Piper didn't really pay attention.

She was too busy staring at Jess and realizing just how very powerful this woman was for a demon to call her one of his own – a demon witch. There weren't very many of them, but when they did happen, it usually didn't bode well for the rest of the world. The universe was prepping for something big – at least that's what all the demon texts she'd read so far had said.

Eisheth picked up the drinks and brought them over to the booth Jess was sitting at, her boots were up on the bench across from her as she sketched something on a piece of paper. The demon handed the hunter her beverage and then kicked her feet off the bench.

Piper's eyes widened when Jess said nothing and Eisheth sat down, pulling Piper with him. She knew they were friends, but she didn't realize just how close until the hunter didn't even seem bothered by that.

"Did Morgan make it home okay?" Piper asked, trying to

see what the hunter was drawing.

"Yeah, I dropped her off at the train station." Jess moved the paper so Piper couldn't see what was on it.

"The train station?"

"She doesn't like planes. Now, what do you think?" Jess slid the paper across the table to Piper and then picked up her coffee cup with a nod of thanks to Eisheth.

Piper studied the scribbles and then realized it was a drawing of her as a stick figure with three stick figure cats climbing all over her. Jess snickered and then flipped the paper over. The other side had an extremely detailed pentagram with specific runes and instructions on it.

Piper rolled her eyes and looked at the symbols used to see what the spell was even for. "It's rather accurate despite the juvenile implications."

Eisheth and Jess chuckled together and the demon hunter and the demon did some complicated handshake Piper pretended to ignore. "Now that you've had them all, what do you think of your mates?" Eisheth asked, resting his elbows on the table, and his chin into his hands like they were schoolgirls dishing gossip.

Piper felt herself blush and cleared her throat, sipping on her coffee. It was delicious. "What is this?" she asked, directing the conversation away from her personal life.

"A raspberry mocha, decaf for you," Eisheth said, sipping his own. "Now if you aren't going to spill the deets on your lover boys, tell me why you summoned me?"

"Well," Piper said, realizing what she held was an unbinding spell tailored for a demon contract. "If I were to make a deal with you for your protection right now, would that negate your deal with the crocs?"

Eisheth shook his head. "No. I'm not hurting you by delivering you."

Piper sighed through her nose, annoyed. She sat back and crossed her arms over her chest. "Thanks for trying to kill that witch by the way."

The demon grinned as he took the top off his cup. He dipped his pinky into the whipped cream and sensually licked it off. "It was my pleasure. Too bad she knows her shit and invoked a protection clause. After the contract is complete though – she's fair game."

The violent promise in those words made Piper shudder, but Jess grinned.

"The Council has allowed me to fight for you Piper, thanks to Morgan's predictions. But I can't do shit until the day of. I even talked to Lucifer who said the rules prevent him from stepping in as Eisheth isn't his." Jess shrugged and then turned. She rested her back against the wall. She stretched her legs out on her bench and then looked at Piper with a rueful smile. "Samael won't step in either, especially not for an unaligned, previously Orthodox Catholic. Eisheth isn't hurting you and won't be, so it's not breaking any rules."

The demon sighed and scooped up more whipped cream with his pinky. "Samael can be such a petty bitch sometimes. He won't even take my calls until all this shit is over."

"I don't think that unbinding spell for Eisheth's contract will work either," Jess said, tapping the paper in Piper's hands. "You won't know for sure until the end of the week though. So you need a backup plan."

Piper folded the spell up and tucked it into her back pocket. "And what if I'm a shifter; could my blood still be used to curse the pride?"

Jess and Eisheth shared a look. "Turning into a cat shifter doesn't change your heritage. It's more about the pharaoh's blood – which is diluted already, but it holds a lot of power. A bit more dilution won't change anything," Eisheth told her, patting her hand in sympathy.

"But it would make you stronger," Jess said. "It's not a bad idea. At the very least you'll be able to bite someone's fucking face off." The mental image made Piper shudder.

Why was nothing ever easy?

"There is one other thing," Piper said slowly.

Jess grinned like she knew what she was about to say, and maybe she did.

"What if I was to create a contract with you Eisheth that started the moment you delivered me to the crocs and your contract with them was done with?" Piper had been thinking about this for a few days now.

The talisman would make it difficult for Eisheth to pop her out and deliver her to Florida unless he ripped the necklace off her. Driving would take too long to meet the deadline, so the only reasonable answer would be boarding a flight. It would only take them a few hours to get to Florida, but there was nothing keeping her mates from coming along. Then all they had to do was take out the crocs.

But Morgan had said if she was delivered...hopefully she didn't mean that literally and was just talking about the spell with her blood.

Eisheth sipped his coffee and Piper picked up her own, wrapping both hands around it for the warmth. "That could work. I assume the contract would be for protection?"

She took a sip and hated herself for what she was about to suggest. "Wouldn't it be easier to just have you kill whoever is there including the witch?"

Eisheth laughed hard at that. "Oh my little queen, how you've grown up." He tugged on her ponytail with affection. "I would love to, but their contract states I cannot murder them until after the spell is over."

Piper slammed her cup down on the table in annoyance, ignoring the drops that splashed onto the surface. "Why is this so fracking difficult? All I want is to go to Crescent City without having to worry about becoming a sacrifice for a spell."

Jess tapped the table with her surprisingly long nails and stared out the window as she sipped her coffee. "I will be there and I will do what I can to keep that from happening, but crocs are really strong and wicked fast. We don't know how many will be there, and there's the dark witch to consider. Eisheth might be able to handle her, but as he said – he can't kill anyone until after the spell is complete which probably means they have something planned for that. I'm assuming it has something to do with your blood."

Piper checked her phone and felt relieved no one had noticed she'd disappeared yet. But she wasn't sure how long this good luck would last.

"The contract states they can't summon me again," Eisheth chimed in. "But that doesn't mean they won't summon someone else. Although...if the witch is dead I doubt they'll survive a second summoning."

Jess waved her hand. "I'll take care of the witch then. I'll need your mates to help fend off the other crocs – they don't have rules against killing them. Eisheth will protect your blood." Jess straightened and leaned onto the table to stare at Piper. "You can have him protect your blood, or you. It will be difficult to do both. The payment will be too high otherwise and you don't want that. Which do you choose?"

Piper glanced at Eisheth who just shrugged. "Balance and rules, darling. If you want both it would cost what you wouldn't want to give up."

"What did the crocs give up?"

He inspected his perfectly manicured nails. "A simple

transportation contract wasn't pricey. They gave me any souls in their pack that were released from their mortal coil before the contract was up. If no one died I got one willing soul to deliver to Samael. But thanks to your lovers I have four now."

Piper didn't know what to think about that. "What's the price to protect my blood?"

Eisheth grinned at her and downed the rest of his coffee. "Oh for you my little queen? Just a drop of that blood."

Jess narrowed her eyes at that request but didn't say anything.

"And for both?"

Eisheth looked uncomfortable. "Nothing you want to give."

"What is it?" she demanded. Desperate times called for desperate measures and for the life of the pride and their future? There was a lot she was willing to give up.

"Something you can't live without," he murmured. "That was Samael's price. Now that could mean anything. It could be your ability to walk so you never dance again. It could be your fertility, your leopard form, your father...you don't want to go down that road, love."

Fucking demons. "Samael's price or yours?" Piper asked softly.

"This shit is on everyone's radar thanks to the consequences, the fucking crocs involving demons, and the witches having to step in," Jess snapped. "The Council approved this job and assigned it to me...not just any hunter. If it was any normal day...Eisheth could ask for a secret as payment, but Samael wants everything he can get out of it."

"Petty bitch," Eisheth murmured, wrapping an arm around Piper's shoulders.

She suddenly felt cold and just wanted to go home, wake up her mates and have them join her in bed so she would be surrounded by them. "I want the contract to be for my blood. Without it the crocs can't curse the Klamath Mountain Pride."

Both Jess and Eisheth looked torn at that. "Are you sure, love?" Eisheth asked gently. "The pride will fall if you are lost regardless. Your mates wouldn't survive it and the remaining leopards would be decimated by the crocs or on the run, looking for a new pride."

Piper sipped her coffee, and then set it down. It was too sweet and she thought she may puke. "I'm sure. No one gets their hands on my blood. You and Samael aren't allowed to use the one drop for anything, and you will protect it with your immortal lives."

Jess's face was serious which made Piper more nervous, but the hunter nodded. "I'll draw up the contract so there's no funny business. It will be exactly what Samael demanded, but within your parameters."

Piper agreed.

"As soon as we get this contract sorted out I'll take care of the blood at the hospital and make sure there's not more anywhere else. Did you ever donate blood?" Eisheth asked.

Piper shook her head. She'd fainted the last time the blood drive came to the university. Needles made her nervous. Eisheth patted her hand sympathetically and turned to Jess.

She watched as Jess and Eisheth haggled over a piece of paper that appeared out of thin air.

This was the right choice. Piper would be able to save the pride. Piper didn't know how many crocs would be there at the ritual thing, but she did know they wouldn't expect her to be a shifter when she got there.

She trusted Caleb, Niko, and Xavier. They would get there in time, and so would Jess and Eisheth. They could do this together and then she would be able to live her life in peace with them in Crescent City. This would all work out.

But no matter how many times she told herself it would be fine...there was a tiny bit of doubt and Piper was terrified one small thing would go wrong and they'd all be royally screwed.

She pricked her finger when it was time and let a drop fall into a tube for Eisheth, and then she signed the contract. Piper had just successfully completed her first deal with a demon and no one had died.

CHAPTER EIGHTEEN

PIPER

Somehow no one had noticed when she'd gotten home or that she was gone. Piper went straight to the shower to wash off the scents of coffee, Jess, and Eisheth. Her mates had cat noses and would know instantly she'd left the apartment.

Piper had planned on this outing for a few days now and she had everything ready. Her clothes went into the bottom of the dirty clothes hamper, and her boots and jacket went deep into her closet. Once the water was running she used her tea tree oil shampoo and conditioner.

Great for her hair and great for covering up pretty much any scent imaginable. Piper even swished mouthwash around while she scrubbed and then spat it out. Someone would hear the shower soon.

"Piper?" Niko asked, peeking his head in.

He was always the most sensitive to her moods and Piper was still freaking out about what she'd just done.

"Another nightmare?" Niko asked, slipping into the shower naked with her.

His arms around her felt delicious and she closed her eyes, leaning back against him. "Something like that," she murmured.

Niko took over washing her hair. He made sure the conditioner covered every strand and then washed it out gently. Piper just wanted to forget everything she'd learned, everything Eisheth and Jess had told her.

Piper turned around and wrapped her arms around Niko's neck and kissed him hard. She shoved her tongue into his mouth and nibbled on his bottom lip, silently begging him to take her offer.

He groaned and gripped her hips tight. His erection pressed against her and Piper wanted him bad. She bent down and licked his cock before turning around and placing her hands on the wall. "I don't want it to be soft," she told him, glancing over her shoulder.

Niko growled at that and pressed against her like they'd done this a thousand times before. He thrust into her hard and fast. It hurt just enough and Piper pushed her ass against him, moaning as he pounded into her.

"Faster Niko, I want you to come so hard you wake everyone else up."

"Christ," he muttered, gripping her hips so hard she knew there would be a perfect impression of his fingers the next morning. "I don't want to come before you," he protested.

"Do as I fucking tell you, Niko. Isn't that why there are three of you?" Piper wanted it rough and hard, she wanted to be in control. There was little else she could control at the moment, but she could make them feel good – she could do that.

Those words made him lose all sense and any control he may have had. Niko yelled her name as he slammed into her one last time and it left her throbbing and aching and needy, but his climax felt so good she instantly relaxed as most of the stress disappeared from her body.

"Piper," Niko murmured, pressing kisses against her back as the water sprayed over the both of them. "Piper, is everything all right?"

He slid out of her and she turned to wrap her arms around him once more. "It is now, thank you." She kissed him gently this time, running her fingers through his hair and just enjoying the sweet taste of him. "I love you, Niko."

He pulled back and searched her eyes as though the words scared him. But when she smiled he hugged her tight. "I love you too, Piper – my mate."

"Could you get Xavier for me?" she asked, hoping this wouldn't be weird for them. "Just Xavier? And then wait for us in the bed?"

Niko didn't question her. He just nodded and gave her another heart-melting kiss. Then he left and Piper closed her eyes under the spray, enjoying the way the water felt as it ran down her body, between her breasts, teasing her sex, and then running down her thighs with Niko's cum.

Another hand touched her breast, cupping it before a warm mouth covered her nipple. Piper gasped as he sucked and the sensation sent a pulse straight to her clit until she was nearly shaking.

She kept her eyes closed but reached for his face, pulling him up so she could kiss him. Those full lips did such terrible things to her. "I love you, Xavier," she whispered as his hand cupped her sex.

"You better," he murmured, slipping a finger inside her. "Because I love you more than anything in this world."

"Show me?" she asked, feeling needy and desperate.

Xavier dropped to his knees and hiked one of her knees up and over his shoulder, exposing her completely to him. The feeling of his mouth against her was electric. She bucked and had to hold onto him as the pressure built slowly.

He took his sweet time, licking and sucking and then he put another finger inside her. God, she wanted it hard and fast, but Xavier wouldn't let her take control. He was way too strong and when her other knee threatened to buckle he threw that one over his other shoulder and lifted her up – just like Caleb had.

Pressing her against the wall he devoured her. Xavier's hot mouth on her shoved her to the edge, but his slow pace kept her from orgasming. She begged, but nothing dissuaded him. Then Caleb suddenly had his hands on her and Xavier passed her over to him, dick so hard and massive it was all she wanted until Caleb thrust inside her.

Piper gasped as he filled her. Caleb was also gentle and slow. "Don't want it hard and fast?" she asked him. Looking into his eyes as she rode him. He held her up, taking all her weight so she didn't get tired. At this pace she could go all night, but that's not what she wanted.

"No babe, I want to make sure you're too tired to have any more nightmares. I would take you out of the shower and lay you down, but that would make you dirty."

"I don't care," Piper said, her fingers tightening in his hair. She trailed her mouth along his jaw, scraping his bristles with her teeth. "Please, take me to bed?"

His growl was more than enough of a response. Suddenly there was cold air and then the feel of her sheets against her skin. Niko was on one side with Xavier and they watched as Caleb took her slowly, sweetly. There was a strange look of awe on their faces, like they'd never thought Caleb could ever be sweet.

But she'd known. The pain of those losses told her how deeply he felt that he had hid it away, tucked behind a stoic mask.

Without her having to say anything Niko shifted so he could watch while he gave Xavier a blowjob. Piper flexed her fingers on Caleb's arms and lifted her hips to meet his. The extra force had her right on the edge. "Please Caleb," she whispered.

Her request had the big alpha growling and swearing as he picked up the pace. Piper felt herself on the edge and then she fell over, throwing her head back as the pleasure completely consumed her. Caleb came with her which only prolonged the sensation until she was nearly limp from it all.

Xavier shouted and Piper watched Niko suck him dry, swallowing everything.

If she wasn't so tired she'd do something about the desire watching that had sparked in her.

"I want you all to claim me before we leave for Crescent City," she murmured, letting Caleb roll them over so he could hold her in his arms.

"Whatever you want, babe. Now go to sleep," Caleb said, smacking her ass gently.

Niko and Xavier chuckled and then snuggled in close just like they had the other night. Piper could easily get used to this. She'd never felt safer than when she had three massive leopard shifters completely surrounding her.

Piper sipped her coffee as she watched Niko show Caleb how to build one of the witch balls of doom. They talked together in low voices and with her human ears she couldn't hear them, but she'd bet a million bucks that Caleb had cracked a joke based on the surprised laugh from Niko. It was wonderful to watch them together.

She scooted to the edge of the couch and inspected the completed Falcon on her coffee table. It was massive, taking up the entire thing at about three feet across. Piper didn't have the heart to take it apart yet so she liked to rearrange the little figures when she noticed one of the boys had changed them from the position she'd left them in last.

Piper snorted when she found Han boinking Leia from behind in the cockpit. "Did you do this?" Piper asked Xavier.

Cat Solo was happily purring in his lap, the traitor.

"Who me? I would never do something so crass," Xavier said in an exaggerated voice. Then he winked and sipped his coffee, scratching Solo's favorite spot behind his ears.

"You just throw them," Niko said and she glanced over at her dining room table again as she rearranged the figures again. "It sends out smoke and this crazy pink electricity that zaps everyone. It's not enough to take anyone out, but it hurts enough to give you a bit of extra time."

"We'll have to keep these away from Charlotte," Caleb muttered.

"Yeah no fucking kidding," Xavier muttered. Then he leaned over her to see what she was doing. "Is that Chewie and...Han? You're so bad." He chuckled and pinched her ass, not hard enough to hurt, but enough she squealed.

The sound instantly brought Caleb and Niko over. Solo growled and hissed at Niko and then retreated to her room, presumably for a nap. Caleb sat on the ground and leaned against her legs while he toyed with one of the droids.

"We'll be packing up and leaving this afternoon," Caleb told her. "You got everything settled for the next week?"

Piper nodded and sat back. Then Niko moved the coffee

table so it was pressed up against her TV. When he knelt in front of her and slid her bottoms down Piper gasped. "I thought we had things to do today."

"Oh we do," Caleb chuckled. "But this is the most important."

"You ready for the claiming ceremony?" Xavier growled softly in her ear as he slid her robe from her shoulders. "Can't be claimed with your clothes on."

"How do you claim someone exactly?" Piper asked, watching with wide eyes as Caleb stood and stripped, quickly followed by Niko.

"Well, all it takes is a bite to claim you. You accept the mate bond, as do we. With cat shifters all three of us need to claim you – it's not comfortable, but the pain won't last long I promise," Caleb explained, tugging her shirt over her head.

Piper had assumed it would be something like that, but still the idea of it made her nervous. "Are you going to bite me as human or cat?"

Xavier stripped next and then all four of them were completely naked and Piper's heart started to pound with nerves, but also desire as she felt how wet and slick she was just from seeing them completely nude.

Niko chuckled. "We can partially shift our teeth so they will be sharper. All we have to do is break the skin and that's it. One bite from only one of us isn't enough. It has to be all three."

She blinked in surprise but nodded.

After deciding this was the route she wanted to go – that she wanted her own strength and power...Piper knew this was the right choice. She knew she wanted to accept the mate bond, but she also knew this was frickin' scary. "Okay let's do this."

"It's not as terrible as it sounds," Caleb murmured, brushing the hair back from her neck. He pressed a kiss to her throat. "We usually do this as a sexual act to ease the pain."

She shivered at those words and her eyes widened as Xavier and Niko came closer. Their hands ran up her legs and trailed over her sensitive center. Piper was captivated by their touch, by the knowledge that at the end of this she would be one of them, and permanently be theirs.

"What do you want, Piper?" Caleb asked.

That damn question again.

"It's my turn for the ass-play," she said breathlessly, kissing first Xavier and then Niko. "I want Caleb inside me, and one of you." Piper shrugged as Caleb pulled her against him so she could feel just how hard he was. "Then one of you takes my mouth. I don't care which."

"Whatever you want, my queen," Caleb murmured into her ear. Then he was sitting on the couch and turning her so she faced him.

Piper felt completely alive for the first time in her life as these three prepared to love her body while they claimed her as theirs. The anticipation – the knowledge that at the end of it she would be bound to them forever...Piper wanted it more than she'd ever wanted anything.

Caleb lounged against the couch and just smiled at her with a cocky alpha smile that made her knees weak. Piper climbed on top of him when he beckoned and she eased slowly down onto his cock, already so wet and ready. His hands on her hips didn't direct her. He let *her* ride *him*. This small allowance had her shaking and she felt her pussy clench around him in response.

Then Xavier had his hand on her ass, spreading her, slicking lube over her asshole, sliding in his pinky to test her.

Piper moaned and slammed against Caleb hard enough he cursed. "Slow down babe, you're not making this easy."

Niko ran his hand up and down her spine, kissing her neck and playing with her nipples while Xavier slowly slid his fingers in and out of her.

"Oh you've definitely played back here before," X murmured, quickening his pace just a little while he slid in another finger. "Our naughty little librarian."

Niko groaned at that and knelt down so he could suck on one nipple and rub his thumb over the other. Piper could barely stand all the sensations at once. All three worked as one, keeping time with her as she ground against Caleb.

Right when she was about to come Caleb stopped her so he could lie on his back on her couch. Xavier's fingers slid out of her and Piper moaned, wanting more. Piper kissed Caleb hard as X climbed up on the couch behind them. She then leaned back to wrap her arm around Xavier's neck, pulling him in for one too. Then she smiled at Niko who was gripping his cock hard.

"While they're both inside me," she said to him. "I want you to claim me."

"Fuck," Niko whispered. "First claim."

Caleb growled in annoyance, but he didn't argue. He just ground her against him until she was on the edge again, dripping all over him. Xavier pressed the head of his cock to her asshole and she slowed down as he moved so carefully.

Piper moaned as he kept sliding in farther and farther, filling her completely and she could feel the strange friction inside as his dick rubbed Caleb's through the thin wall separating them. "Now you all are first at something," she said, panting as Caleb and Xavier timed their thrusts to match and she pulsed, ready to explode.

Niko came over and ran a hand up her leg, over her ass, along the curve of her spine, and then held the back of her neck. He angled her head ever so slightly and then pressed his mouth to her skin. Piper gasped in anticipation, feeling the flicker of anxiety and anticipation like she did every time she got a shot.

First he kissed her, and then licked the spot tenderly. Caleb's thumb went to her clit and she moaned. That's when Niko bit down and the sharp sting hurt. He licked the blood she could feel trickling down, and her heart rate picked up as her skin began to tingle strangely.

Any residual pain disappeared when Caleb and Xavier picked up their paces, distracting her with the pleasure. Then suddenly Xavier took her hand and brought her wrist to his mouth at the same time Caleb sat up, carefully adjusting all three of them with his impressive strength.

Piper watched as Xavier and Caleb shared a look – it was deep and meaningful and downright hot as they held each other's gaze and together they bit down. Caleb claimed a breast and Xavier her wrist. It didn't feel great, but Niko distracted her by taking her mouth. He wrapped his hand around the back of her neck and kissed her like it might be the last time he ever saw her – like they may not make it through whatever came next.

Then X and Caleb were both pounding into her again and she screamed as she came. The sensation of both of them inside her was everything she'd thought it would be and more. Piper collapsed on top of Caleb's chest, completely spent.

But then reached out for Niko.

He obliged and she pulled him into her mouth as she lay on top of Caleb. Niko's cock was close enough to the big Alpha he reached over and grabbed Niko's balls gently while Piper swirled her tongue around him.

Caleb and Xavier worked themselves inside of her until she was about ready to shatter again. She sucked hard, wrapping her hand around Niko so she could control him better. When he came in her mouth, bucking at both her and Caleb's touch, she kept sucking until Niko's knees went weak.

Then Xavier thrust into her and shouted her name, filling her ass and Caleb hardened at the sensation. She could feel how close he was just by the way he stretched her even more. Xavier pulled out and collapsed on the couch and Niko slumped next to him.

Then suddenly Caleb lifted her up and flipped her over until he had her bent over the arm of the couch. He pounded into her and she screamed for him. The moment he came she did too, feeling completely exhausted and satisfied.

All three of them had made their claim.

The strange tingling on her skin settled into her bones and then disappeared. Piper checked her wrist and saw it was completely healed. It was just a glittering white scar like the cut Morgan had healed.

When the mate bond snapped into place she gasped. All three of them were tied to her, like an anchor in her chest with three ropes wrapped around it. If she plucked one it would lead her to the mate on the other side. Piper rolled over when Caleb pulled out and looked at the three of them.

Piper grinned. "Well at least the couch is leather."

All three of them laughed and wrapped their arms around her. Piper loved how they didn't shy away from each other – how Caleb was slowly getting used to the other two. She could see the way they were forming into a solid unit and Piper adored it.

"Let's get you cleaned up," Xavier said. "Then I'll make something to eat before we pack up and go."

Piper was too happy to argue. She wanted a nap and more

time to cuddle with them, but she supposed they could do that at the house in Crescent City. Soon she would be safe and they would have a few days before chaos ensued. She planned to enjoy every moment until then.

CHAPTER NINETEEN

CALEB

"So I found this spell, and I thought we could try it out real fast?" Piper said with a piece of paper in her hand.

Her hair was still wet and she smelled like tea tree and coconut with a hint of her natural lotus blossom scent. Beneath all of that was the blooming scent of leopard. She would be able to shift soon and then they could all go running together through the property.

Caleb touched a stray curl. He couldn't believe she was theirs. That this was going to be his future.

"Caleb?" she asked, smiling a little.

"Yes, if the spell doesn't take long we can do it now."

Xavier chuckled as he passed by with two bags in his hands. His shoulder brushed Caleb's and for the first time ever he didn't bristle at the contact. Feeling the other leopard inside Piper with him – it had been a life changing experience.

All three of them were in this together. And now that

they'd officially made their claim he felt a slight tether to the other two as well as the strong anchor of Piper in the center of their triangle – the strongest shape in nature.

Niko came over with Cat Solo in his arms to peer at the spell. The two had come to some kind of strange truce which may have something to do with Piper's scent all over him. "What's this?" he asked, pointing to the underside of the spell.

Piper blushed. "It's nothing. Do we have everything we need for the spell, Niko?"

"Is that us crawling all over you?"

Caleb turned the paper over and then laughed. It certainly was them. Their mate was so delightful. "We should have everything on here."

Niko nodded. "It doesn't call for a specific phase of the moon, or time of day so we can do it right now if you want. Let me get the supplies." Then suddenly Cat Solo reared up and attacked Niko's hand, making the leopard curse and drop the domestic. "For fuck's sake, and here I was thinking we'd made progress."

Piper covered her mouth as she laughed, watching the two of them.

"Here, be useful," Niko teased, tossing her the chalk. "Sketch that pentagram exactly as it is on your coffee table."

Caleb watched her kneel down and start moving the Falcon. Christ...this woman was his mate – and soon she'd be one of two females in his pride. He was the luckiest Alpha alive. Somehow he'd managed to bring his pride back from the brink of death and all it took was one hard as nails woman to give him the hope to do it.

"Who did this to the porgs?!" Piper shouted, pulling the weird-looking creatures from the exhaust ports.

He chuckled and kissed the top of her head. "I promise it

wasn't me. I'm going to help Xavier pack up. Need anything else, darlin'?"

Piper didn't look up as she carefully set the Falcon onto the ground. "It was you wasn't it Niko."

"They're weird!" Niko yelled from the kitchen.

Piper shook her head and started on the sketch for the pentagram. She shook her head and smiled. "No, I think I'll survive despite the atrocities you three commit on these poor characters. Just don't forget Cat Solo or that box of books." She pointed to the box in the corner and then finished a rune.

"I'm not sure we should bring demon texts."

That sassy little look she threw him made him melt inside but Caleb crossed his arms over his chest and kept his face straight.

"Eisheth will take them back for me if I can't get them to the library in time," she said. "And not all of them are demon texts."

"We have a witch library in Crescent City," Caleb protested. He did not like the energy most of them gave off and they weren't from his territory.

Piper mumbled under her breath, something unpleasant no doubt since she made sure it was in a language he didn't understand. "This pentagram has to be done in a specific order, could you be quiet?"

Caleb gritted his teeth. He wanted to smack her ass and kiss her at the same time. It was a confusing confliction. He went and grabbed the box of books, noticing a few romance novels in there among the demon lore and shifter history – there were a few other books about the Hellenic Period as well.

He would never be bored with Piper around.

"You two finish up the spell and we'll leave in about an

hour," Caleb told Niko as his beta passed with witchy looking objects in his arms and Cat Solo on his heels.

"No problem boss. It'll be nice to be back in our own territory again."

Caleb couldn't agree more. Having to request permission for every single little thing grated on his nerves and made him irritable – well more than normal. Fuck, Piper had changed that too. He could feel the difference as he left the apartment.

He no longer felt the urge to rip anything and everything apart at a moment's notice.

"Are they still doing witch stuff?" Xavier asked as Caleb approached his truck.

His Second rested his arms on the truck bed and glared back at the apartment. His dislike for all things witchy was a bit amusing when it didn't annoy Caleb. "Yeah, they should be done within the hour though."

He tossed the box of books into the bed of his truck and started securing all their stuff.

"Hey! We don't *throw* demon books. You and Piper man, testing fucking fate around here at every turn." Xavier rearranged the disheveled books and then tucked the box gently into the corner.

The whole thing made Caleb laugh and Xavier looked up in surprise. He understood why. It had been years since he could laugh about anything really.

"She's been good for you," Xavier said, pulling the tailgate down and hopping up. "I've never seen you so not-cranky." He patted the space next to him and Caleb hesitated. "Come on, I won't bite unless you ask."

Caleb rolled his eyes at that and then sat next to the man who'd been his lifelong rival. Both of them had always been incredibly competitive, and Xavier was dominant enough to be Alpha if Caleb hadn't been born an Alpha to the then current Alpha of the pride.

It still surprised him he'd never challenged him. "Can I ask you something?"

Xavier glanced sideways at him but nodded.

"Why didn't you ever try to take the pride from me?"

His Second shrugged and watched a car park. "You've always done a good job. I couldn't even protect my mom. How was I going to protect an entire pride?"

Caleb hesitated and then he slung an arm around Xavier's shoulders. "You were just a kid, X. I trust you to protect the pride. It's why you're my Second, not just because you're the most dominant out of the others. I trust you to protect our mate."

The tension between them from a lifetime of rivalry and dominance games eased even further when Xavier glanced at him and nodded. Caleb said nothing about the wet sheen in his eyes and Xavier said nothing about the arm around his shoulders.

"She's going to be a handful," Xavier said, changing the subject.

He smiled at that. "I can't wait, to be honest. What do you think she's going to do first when we get home?"

"Probably spend all day in the estate's library. Then she'll probably ask to shift."

Caleb nodded at that. "We need to help her through that first shift before the end of the week. I want to train her in her leopard form as much as we can before shit goes down."

"Sounds good to me." Xavier laid back and cushioned his head with his hands as they waited.

Xavier wouldn't go back into the apartment until the witch stuff was done, and Caleb decided he would keep him company until then. The sun was nice and warm after all and it relaxed the tightness in his muscles. He closed his eyes and breathed in deep, tasting and scenting everything he could on the air.

Claiming Piper had been a fucking dream, and if he didn't still taste her blood on his tongue he almost wouldn't believe it had happened. Caleb leaned back too and laced his fingers over his stomach. Soon they would be on their way home and he could show his mate everything about his life.

Fuck, he'd even agreed to compete in the tango for her. Well, practicing would certainly be fun. Caleb had always enjoyed his dance lessons, but with Piper? He'd use any excuse to put his hands on her.

"You two taking a fucking catnap?" Niko demanded, tossing a bag onto Xavier's stomach so the other male had the air knocked out of him.

"Don't be jealous," Caleb mumbled. "You can nap on the way back if you want."

"Fine, I get the backseat with Piper."

Xavier grumbled but got up and took the rest of the bags from Niko. "You guys got everything?"

Caleb sat up and saw Piper with Cat Solo in his carrier. She clutched it to her chest. His mate was nervous and smelled like magic. Caleb wrinkled his nose and pulled her to him. "Everything will be okay," he told her.

Piper nodded and kissed his cheek before she climbed into the back of the cab. Cat Solo went in the middle and he could hear Niko grumble about the carrier. Caleb smiled and knocked X off the tailgate. "Let's go back home."

They all piled into the truck and he felt a huge weight lift from his chest as they pulled out of her apartment complex. There would be more room at the estate and they would have their protections both magic and non to help keep Piper safe.

Her father would be by in a few days to come take a look at some houses and talk to the chief of police. Caleb would be glad when everything was settled.

Only half a week more though and the demon contract would force Eisheth to deliver her. Well, Caleb would be interested in seeing if the demon could get through their perimeter. And if he could...that was a problem for another day.

The drive was quiet as they headed north. It would be about four hours until he was back in his territory, but about five or six before they pulled up to the pride's house. Caleb glanced in the rearview mirror and watched Piper snuggle up with Niko. Cat Solo was moved to the floor so she could stretch out.

A nap would do her some good after the claiming.

He ran through his mental checklist. Moving her to Crescent City would be a bit of work. Then Caleb had to talk to the Mayor and Chief of Police about available positions as a police officer so they were prepared for Piper's dad, and then get in touch with his realtor – a sweet little bobcat who always came to him with new properties before they hit the market. She wasn't officially in his pride, but he watched out for her while she decided where she wanted to live.

Caleb drove for hours in amiable silence with the others. The second he hit the freeway Piper had fallen asleep. He took the I-5 to the 299 and then to the 101 freeway. It was inconvenient to get home from Sacramento, but Caleb was just glad to be headed home. His Third was familiar with running the basic pride requirements, but he never enjoyed it.

The Mad River was one of the natural borders of his territory and Caleb felt anxious to cross. Arcata was just south of what was his and the second he crossed into McKinleyville they would be in Klamath territory.

Caleb signaled to get over so he could get onto the 101. There weren't very many people on the road thankfully since it was in the middle of a weekday, but still he made sure to drive the speed limit. Cops had nothing better to do and his mate was in the car.

Then he slammed into something that felt like a cement wall.

Time slowed as the truck crumbled against an invisible force. Piper screamed and Caleb felt his heart thunder in his chest as he tried to assess the situation while every millisecond mattered. But he was still stuck in his confusion. What the actual fuck had he even hit?

Then the truck tried to flip and Cat Solo yowled, but it was like there was a wall in front of him and they weren't going anywhere. Other cars honked and screeched around him as Caleb forced open the driver's side door with his supernatural strength.

Piper – he had to make sure she was alive. Thank fucking god she had shifter healing now, but still. Caleb ripped open her door and blood was all he smelled. "Piper!"

The entire cab was crumbled to the point that he was fucking shocked no one was dead. There were four heartbeats including the cat's. Xavier shoved open his door and tumbled out of the front seat and onto the asphalt. His Second would secure the area even if he was just as desperate as Caleb to touch her, make sure she was alive.

Niko had his arm around her, probably the only thing that kept her from flying through the windshield and that arm looked broken, but he was unconscious at the moment which was a small mercy.

Piper blinked at him in confusion until she realized what had happened. She struggled to get out while Caleb ran his hands over her, checking for broken bones.

"I'm stuck, Caleb. My legs."

It was all he could do to keep from roaring as he ripped the front seats out of the cab.

Piper was murmuring something he couldn't understand, but all he could focus on was her. "Are you hurt anywhere?" he asked. "Where are you bleeding?"

Glass was everywhere and he and Xavier had borne the brunt of it, but he could smell her blood.

"I don't know," she mumbled. The smell of her fear was strong and it made him violent. His mate was hurt.

Finally he had the leverage to pull her out as he ripped out the last piece of the front bench. Caleb scooped her up and cradled her to his chest. She held on to him, burying her face in his neck as he pulled her out. It fucking broke his heart. He looked up and saw Niko was still unconscious.

"X! Get Niko out of the cab. I need to make sure nothing's broken." Caleb set Piper down on the ground so she could lean against the front wheel and then ran his hands over her again, checking for anything that wasn't as it should be, any cuts, or bruising. As long as there was nothing internal they should be okay.

"Caleb there's nothing there," Piper said, pointing. She stared at the truck and the way it looked like it was smashed up against something. But she was right, there was nothing fucking there.

That didn't bode well.

Satisfied she was okay – just bruised with a few cuts – Caleb set her against the tire and put Cat Solo and his carrier in her arms. The cat was yowling up a storm and clearly fine thanks to his carrier. "Stay here," he said. "I'm going to take a look."

He jogged over and there was physically nothing he could see. He reached out and felt the crackle of magic when his hand hit something solid. Following it he realized it went along his territory line. Someone had fucking blocked off his territory and it only affected him and probably the other two. Cars were driving through just fine.

A few people had stopped to watch, take videos, or call someone – he didn't know and he didn't care. He just needed to figure out what the hell was going on now that he knew everyone was okay.

There was a slight 'pop' sound and the hair on the back of his neck rose in warning.

Caleb whirled around just in time to see someone appear out of thin air, rip the talisman off Piper's neck, and grab her hand. He ran straight for her, shouting at Xavier, but he was too slow. His fingers just barely brushed the fabric of the demon's suit and then passed through nothing but air as he leapt. Caleb landed hard on the asphalt.

"What the hell?" Xavier demanded, Niko's arm over his shoulder. Then his Second realized Piper was gone.

"Who the fuck was that?" Caleb snarled. He grabbed the talisman from the ground and roared. He was furious. His leopard was so close to the surface he wanted to rip his clothes off and shift right there.

He'd known this could happen. Caleb had *known* that he may not be enough to keep her safe.

"Calm down, kitty cat."

Caleb whirled around and reached for the demon, but Eisheth popped out of existence and then reappeared farther away. The demon looked at the magic field in distaste and then at the cars slowing down to see what was going on.

Sirens in the distance told him someone had finally called 911, but he didn't fucking care. "Take me to her now. You were supposed to be the one to deliver her," Caleb accused. "How could you let this happen?"

He wanted to shift and chase down his mate until he could tear every single croc to pieces, starting with that fucking demon. Caleb desperately wanted to track her, but there was no trail to follow. She'd been transported through a different plane.

Without Eisheth he would never find her.

"What do you want?" Xavier asked. "Whatever it is I'll give it to you."

Eisheth slipped one hand into his pocket and inspected the nails of the other. "Seems the crocs got impatient and made a deal with Forneus, the fucking bastard. But don't worry, your little queen already made a deal with me, leopard. She bargained for the protection of her blood so it could never be used to curse you or the pride. I believe a simple transportation for backup would fall under this bargain, but first." He snapped his fingers and every cut, bruise, and ache from the crash was gone from all three of their bodies. "You don't owe me anything for this."

Niko breathed a sigh of relief when his arm was back to normal, and then he snarled, reaching for the demon.

But Eisheth just teleported and appeared next to the cat carrier. He held out one hand and they all watched in shock as drops of blood flew through the air from the cab and the asphalt until it was a tiny liquid ball and then...ash. The blood became nothing but ash.

The whole thing scared the shit out of Caleb. She'd gone and made a deal with a demon for him and the pride.

Eisheth grabbed Cat Solo. "I'll get him to your house, and then I'll be back to take you to her. Call a witch team for this and call Jess. We have shit to do."

Caleb was too angry to say anything. Of course she'd slipped out at some point, or summoned Eisheth while they were asleep. Of *course* she fucking bargained for the pride and not her life. Oh, he would spank the shit out of her when they got her back.

There was no 'if.' He would get her back if it was the last thing he did.

CHAPTER TWENTY

PIPER

By this point she knew what it felt like to be yanked through time and space, but Piper hadn't had it last so long before. When she could breathe again she was gasping and fell to her knees the moment the unfamiliar demon released her.

Well, the unbinding spell obviously hadn't worked especially since this demon wasn't Eisheth.

She reached for the talisman, but it wasn't there. Somehow he'd known where it was. Who could possibly have told him? Thankfully he'd left her Egyptian necklace, but Piper had no idea if that would actually be able to help her or not.

It wasn't her only protection. If she could figure out how to shift...she had just been claimed, but had no idea how to turn leopard. Christ on a cracker, she was supposed to have at least three more days to learn how to shift.

"Piper Leigh Kostopoulos," the demon said in a silky smooth voice. "You have been delivered."

Then someone grabbed her and shoved her into someone else's arms.

Piper was still just trying to get air in her lungs, but the hands on her sent chills down her spine. Her senses were heightened after the claiming, and she smelled...what was that? Fish, and what she would imagine a pond would smell like, or maybe a swamp?

Shit, she was in trouble.

Trying to escape whoever held her was fruitless. Their grip was immovable and hurt more when she struggled. Finally Piper went limp. It would make more sense to figure out how many of them there were, where she was...she hoped to god Eisheth had shown up to the car accident. She'd texted him rather desperately and then she had disappeared, but her phone was still back at the truck, or what was left of the vehicle.

Someone had put a barrier around the Klamath Pride territory that much was clear.

Piper peered through her hair at the crocs surrounding her, talking to the demon who'd delivered her. A woman stood off to the side, sketching something onto the concrete floor. She couldn't get a good look at her, but it must be the dark witch Piper had heard so much about.

The demon snapped his fingers and Piper instantly felt all her aches and pains disappear. When she looked down all her cuts were healed and she saw she was wearing a red dress with a black corset over it. The demon smiled at her, but it wasn't pleasant. "Might as well make her look pretty for the sacrifice," he said. "The paltry amount of blood from those cuts wouldn't be enough for anything anyway."

"Thanks Forneus, you can have your pick of souls," one of the crocs said.

Forneus...that was the demon Eisheth had mentioned.

Piper looked around, trying to figure out where she was – if there was any way to escape. There were four men she didn't recognize who all had a certain look about them, plus the one holding her. Then there was the witch. It looked like they were in some kind of basement, or...a parking garage? Were they really in a parking garage? How tacky.

The air felt muggy and hot. She was already sweating and Piper assumed they weren't in California anymore. If she had to take a guess they were somewhere in Florida, but she'd never been so she couldn't say for sure.

"I think I'll take *your* soul," Forneus said with that sharp grin.

"I'm the Alpha," the croc snapped. "The contract states you can't take my soul."

"Hm...then maybe I'll take your son's. I just want the soul of an Alpha."

At that the shifter paled and no matter how much Piper hated the crocs for doing this to her she gasped in horror. This demon wasn't like Eisheth at all.

"Then you can have my soul, but only after I die from natural causes or from the blood feud."

The demon winked at Piper and then walked around the pentagram the witch was drawing. She ignored him like he didn't matter and that frightened Piper even more. This witch had survived Eisheth and wasn't worried about Forneus. How much power did she have exactly?

"Too bad you didn't state that in the contract. Seems your little witch doesn't give a shit about you as much as you thought she did," Forneus mused. "Although if you like...I'll take a pint of Piper's blood in payment instead."

Why the hell did everyone want her blood so badly?

"Done. We only needed two pints for this spell. Now get out of my way."

The Alpha grabbed for her and Piper snarled – actually snarled at him. The look of surprise on the croc's face would have been comical if she could actually shift and do something to protect herself. But she had to save any chance of that for when the others showed.

Where the hell were Jess and Eisheth with her mates?

The croc Alpha grabbed for her again and she kicked at him, pulling against the strangers arms. "Why do you want to curse the pride?" she asked when he finally got a hold of her and yanked her to his face.

"You may have just been claimed by a leopard, but you will pay for what they've done with your life," he told her. That gravelly voice was cold and heartless despite the emotion she'd seen on it when the demon had mentioned his son.

"Please, you don't have to do this," she pleaded as he dragged her over to the witch.

Then she saw the iron shackles on the wall right above the pentagram. Piper knew then that they planned to bleed her dry. It was all her blood or nothing, especially since it seemed to be so precious.

The other crocs crossed their arms over their chest and ignored her. Piper wouldn't get anywhere with them. "Why *my* blood?" she asked the demon instead while the Alpha closed those shackles around her wrists.

Forneus came within biting distance and she seriously considered it until he grinned at her, showing sharp teeth that reminded her of some kind of deep sea creature. Piper recoiled, but didn't take her eyes off him. "Didn't anyone tell you?" He leaned in then and whispered in her ear. "Pharaoh's blood has enough power to open one of the Seven Seals of Hell. I have a few friends I promised to get out about a millennia ago."

Her heart stopped beating for a moment as she took that in. Her blood...could do that? No wonder so many outside sources wanted in on this. What happened here today – it could change the world. *This* was why Jess had been assigned her case.

The knowledge didn't make her feel any better. It made her feel worse if that were even possible.

Then the witch stood up and dusted the chalk off her hands. Piper was finally able to see what she'd been drawing and...it terrified her. She had never seen a pentagram so complex and detailed. The witch had to have been working on it for hours and it was flawless.

As a scholar she was impressed. The demon texts all said the more complex the pentagram the more power required to cast it. And this was a demon spell – not a normal witch one. Somehow this witch had enough power to pull this off without any help from a demon.

Yup, Piper was officially scared of her.

"Circe, are you ready to do the honors?" Forneus asked, holding his hand out for the witch.

The name made Piper do a double take. She looked the witch in the face for the first time and realized it was the very same witch who'd given her the talisman. *That* was how Forneus knew. What a bitch.

Circe smiled at Piper. "Being neutral is boring. This was way more fun."

Morgan had trusted her, and Piper had trusted Morgan. Why do this? "What do you get out of it?" Piper asked. How could this possibly benefit her?

"Enough!" the Alpha croc snapped. "Let's get this done already."

"There has to be a way to work this out!" Piper yelled as Circe walked away, and in her wake she felt that power stir, terrifying her. "We could end the blood feud if you'd just be willing to sit down and talk with us."

All five crocs laughed at her.

"Baby girl," the Alpha said gently, almost like he regretted this whole thing. "It's been going on for over two hundred years. You've been aware of it for a week and a half and you want us to what, kiss and make up? There are too many dead on both sides for us to let this go."

Piper pulled at her restraints. She needed to get free, or shift, or...shit she was in trouble. Circe started mumbling and held her hands up as she did so. If her mates didn't come soon Piper would be dead.

Where were Eisheth and Jess? Had they betrayed her like Circe had Morgan? Or were they doing as she'd asked? It was impossible to know in her current situation and that terrified her. Piper felt so helpless, so weak compared to all these powerful people and she knew without help there was no way out of this for her.

Circe closed her eyes and her voice grew louder as the power in the room built. Piper could feel it on her skin like air right before lightning struck. The magic tasted metallic and she pulled against the shackles with all her new strength and still they held. That's when she saw the incantations etched into the metal.

Well...at least she'd tried. There was one last thing she could do, but Piper didn't know what would happen if she tried to shift while shackled in enchanted iron. Probably nothing good. She felt despair rushing up to swallow her whole. No one had come for her, or if they were they were going to be too late.

As the spell went on Piper felt her necklace warm and it gave her a small shred of hope. There might be a chance to hold them off until Eisheth could arrive with her mates.

But then Circe came forward with a wicked looking knife in one hand and she went straight for Piper's neck. Her necklace flared and the witch cursed. Piper used that opportunity to kick as hard as she could. The light from her necklace blinded her, but she heard the knife clatter to the ground.

Then suddenly someone was touching her and she snarled.

"It's me babe," Xavier whispered. "I'm sorry, we had to wait for the perfect moment. It's a good thing Niko was right about your necklace having real magic."

Relief flooded her so hard and so fast Piper sagged against the shackles. He cut through the metal and she fell into his arms when they finally released. The sound of snarls and screams filled the parking garage and she was almost too afraid to look after what had happened in the library.

But Piper needed to see. She looked up and saw Jess holding Circe by the throat. She lifted the woman up and the sheer power and force required to do that astounded Piper. Whatever Circe was, she was nothing compared to a demon witch.

Then the woman just...disintegrated. Her entire body turned into ash. When Jess turned to look at Piper her eyes glowed – they literally glowed with hellfire. Piper shuddered; eternally grateful this hunter was on her side.

Eisheth was there as well, throwing nasty-looking magic at Forneus. The two were well matched and wicked fast as they popped in and out of existence to avoid each other and the curses.

Xavier helped Piper stand and she looked up to see Caleb grab a croc and literally tear his arm off to keep him from grabbing Niko. And Niko in leopard form was pure, violent poetry. He shook one of the crocs by the neck hard enough to snap and then went for the next one.

But then the crocs shifted. One of them clamped down on Niko's leg while another went after Caleb while they were occupied.

"Go," she told Xavier, pushing him off her. "Go help them before everyone is dead."

He gave her one long look and then handed her a gun and a knife. "Don't let anyone near you," Xavier said. "We'll take care of this."

She nodded and cursed Forneus and his timing. A few more days and she'd at least know how to shift into a leopard.

Jess went after a croc, but he was insanely fast in his animal form, dodging the hunter at every opportunity until she just...jumped on his back, wrapping an arm around its throat and another over its head like Piper had seen people do on animal documentaries.

When Jess muttered under her breath the croc was force-shifted back to human and without hesitation she snapped his neck. It was awful but Piper couldn't look away. Never had she seen so much violence in her life.

Then a crocodile ran at her. Piper shot without hesitation, not even thinking about what she was doing. All those days at the gun range with her father had paid off and it dropped to the ground in a heap, a bullet-hole through its head.

Piper heaved, throwing up everything she'd eaten that day. The guy had just tried to sacrifice her, but she'd taken a life. She forced herself to watch as he shifted back into a human. Piper memorized his face.

She told herself this had been survival. Piper had done what she had to do to stay alive. If the croc hadn't taken her, hadn't tried to kill her twice – he'd still be alive.

It didn't make her feel much better, but it did give her a

grim determination. If one of these bastards came at her or her mates she wouldn't hesitate then either. Piper would choose an alternate path if she could, but this was her life now.

A snarl and then a yowl made her whip around. Piper saw the biggest leopard was under two crocs. Caleb must have shifted at some point. A second leopard was bleeding on the floor, unable to stand or help. The second was trying to get the soft underbelly of one of the crocs – she assumed Niko was the one who was hurt so this had to be Xavier.

Caleb was dying under those two crocs as they shook him. Piper could see it as his chest heaved, trying to breathe.

Jess was too busy with Eisheth and Forneus. There was no one to help them. Piper knew if she didn't do something and fast she was going to lose Caleb, if not him *and* Niko. There was no way she was going to allow that to happen.

Piper stepped forward, ready to shoot another croc, but she fell to all fours instead. Then she opened her eyes and everything looked different. The world seemed bled dry of color with only a few left – like watching a film in sepia tone. When she went to step forward she stumbled and Piper looked down to see paws instead of feet.

She'd shifted.

Somehow her desperation had helped her slip from one body to the next.

If she could have smiled she would have. Instead she ran straight for the crocs attacking her mates and let her instincts take over. Piper bit down on one croc's tail as hard as she could and he whipped around to face her, releasing Caleb.

Now that she had his attention she didn't know what to do and Piper froze, panicking.

The croc snapped at her and she moved. Suddenly she was running, trying to sort through all the new sounds and smells and the strange colors of the world.

"Whoa there, kitty cat," Eiseth exclaimed when she darted around him. He had Forneus in a strong hold while Jess tied him up with what looked and smelled like enchanted zip cuffs.

She dashed for Caleb who had managed to get free from the other croc. Between him and Xavier the croc was ravaged and in pieces before she could blink. Piper ran toward them, hoping they'd be able to get the one on her ass.

Niko was still hurt and laying on the floor in a heap. Piper was scared whatever was wrong would be something irreparable. The smell of her mates' blood on the air made her panic and it was impossible to focus on any one thing. Piper stumbled as she reached Caleb and as one, he and Xavier turned on the croc chasing her.

Suddenly the croc realized his mistake and tried to run from her mates. But they were on him in a flash. Piper looked away from the carnage, just glad to be alive even if she felt shaky and unsure in this new form. She had no idea how to turn back into a human.

Piper slunk over to Niko and sniffed his leg, which had a bone sticking out of it and blood was everywhere. If she'd been human she probably would have puked again. He lifted his head up and looked at her with such tired and pained eyes. Piper rubbed her head against his jaw and then curled around him.

At least Niko was still alive. She would protect him until the others took care of the danger.

With all the crocs dead but one, Piper knew they'd managed to avoid disaster – just barely. But she'd killed someone. Four crocs and a witch and one of them had a son. It made her so incredibly sad. She felt desolate inside. Piper knew it had been survival – her pride or their group – but it didn't mean she liked how it had turned out.

She released a massive sigh and rested her head on Niko's back. There had to be something they could do to end this blood feud. Piper didn't want to have to wonder if she was going to lose one of them one day to an attack. There had to be a way.

Then that other croc's heart stopped and she knew it was over. Xavier and Caleb loped over to her and Niko.

Eisheth and Jess had Forneus and as soon as they took care of him...it would all be over.

CHAPTER TWENTY-ONE

PIPER

E isheth clapped his hands while Jess wrangled Forneus. "This turned out even better than I'd hoped."

Piper didn't lift her head, but she did glare at him. Her mates were severely hurt and she couldn't turn back into a human.

The demon sighed. "Fine, one last time just so you don't get any ideas and chew on my favorite shoes, my little queen." Eisheth snapped his fingers and Niko's leg was completely healed. The blood matted on his fur was gone and she couldn't smell...any blood at all.

The crocs were no more than piles of ash and Caleb and Xavier looked perfect. Then suddenly they were naked men and rushing to help her. The soft body below her had skin instead of fur and Niko's gentle murmurs as he stroked her back shocked her.

Piper backed away, not sure how she felt being touched in her cat form yet.

"Babe, it's okay," Caleb told her, but he was just so big as he bent over, reaching out for her.

Then Xavier got down on one knee and held his hand out for her as well. "All you have to do is think about what it feels like to be human. Remember the colors you could see, the way wind feels in your hair, sunlight on your skin, and then close your eyes."

"We're here for you," Niko whispered. "All three of us."

Piper closed her eyes as Xavier had suggested. Then Caleb's deep, warm voice was so soothing to her sensitive ears when he murmured, "Darlin' the three of us will always be here, forever. We're not going anywhere without you. We love you, please – just trust us."

Then the world sounded different and she opened her eyes. Piper gasped when the riot of color was back and she checked her paws/hands. All five digits were there. Then she realized she was naked. Piper covered herself with a squeak. Her mates were naked too, but they clearly weren't worried about it with all those abs and rippling muscles.

"I got this," Eisheth muttered. Another snap of his fingers and she was in a long, flowy sundress.

Piper thanked him and then she realized all her mates were clothed too. For some reason that made her blush. "That was weird," she said.

All three of them smiled at her and pulled her in for a hug. Then she kissed each and every one of them as thoroughly as possible. She thought for a moment she was going to lose one if not all of them. Piper hadn't realized until that moment just how insanely intertwined her life was with theirs now.

The idea of living without any one of them...it was soul crushing. There was so much despair waiting for her at the end of that thought that Piper finally understood exactly what

Caleb meant by going feral. It would certainly be better than living without them, because it wouldn't really be living if they weren't by her side.

"Is it really over?" she asked. "No one else will come for my blood?"

Caleb shook his head. "It's over for now. That was the Alpha of all the crocs in Florida. By the time they regather the Council will be on their shit."

"You still have me," Eisheth said. "I have to protect your blood indefinitely." He inspected his nails and sighed like he hadn't agreed to this willingly. "I could kill everyone who knows, but it'll just be easier to take those memories. Don't worry about that."

Caleb nodded. "The blood feud isn't over, but I'm hoping with a new Alpha we might be able to try and get a truce. You never know." He shrugged and looked down at her. "Crazier things have happened."

Piper hoped he was right. It was something she planned to address as soon as she'd found her place in the pack. The life of the croc she'd killed weighed heavily on her, but she saw now what her mates had meant when they'd told her they were willing to do anything to keep her alive.

Everything was different when her life, or the lives of her mates were at stake.

"You did so well," Caleb told her. "You shifted all on your own."

"Yeah," Xavier agreed, helping her to her feet. "You bit the shit out of that crocs tail, and let me tell you what. Charlotte, the kitten, did that to me once and it fucking hurts."

That made Piper laugh despite everything. "Charlotte bites your tail?"

Niko pulled her in for a hug so it was just the two of them.

"She is the little baby for the entire pride. You'll get to meet her soon," he murmured into her hair. Then he kissed her. It was long and slow and toe curling. Piper melted against him and breathed in his scent. Then Niko pulled away so he could look into her eyes. "Thank you for protecting me."

Piper was dazed and all she could do was nod. That had been some kiss.

And as if Xavier knew that was exactly what she was thinking he pulled her in for one of his own, slipping his silky tongue into her mouth while he slid his hands into her hair. "Yes, thank you for helping us. Without you we might not have made it."

Then Caleb pulled her over to him and he wrapped his arms around her, pulling her up as he kissed her hard. It was a kiss she would never forget as he forced her mouth open so he could taste her. He nipped her lip and she couldn't help the groan she made. "Delicious," he murmured.

"Fucking gross. Shifters and their goddamn PDA. Let's get the hell out of here. I've got better things to do," Jess snapped, shaking Forneus who just grumbled.

Piper didn't look away from Caleb but she nodded. When he released her she felt a bit lightheaded from their attentions, but had enough sense to turn to Jess. "Thank you for everything," she told her. "No offense, but I hope I never see you again."

The demon hunter just grinned. "None taken, but I might pop in to the next West Coast Pride barbecue over the Fourth of July. Good luck, Piper Leigh Kostopoulos." Jess winked and then popped out of existence.

Piper blinked as she realized Jessica James could teleport. She didn't want to know why the hunter chose to ride around on a motorcycle. So she smiled at Eisheth – a demon, but a friend as well. He'd come through for her when she'd needed it most. "Thank you for getting them here."

The demon actually blushed as he slipped his hands in his pockets and shrugged. "It was nothing. Also, Cat Solo is at the pride's estate, safe and sound. You ready to get out of Florida, my little queen? It's awfully muggy here. It's doing some pretty terrible things to your hair."

Piper smiled and nodded. "Yeah, let's go home." And when she said it, she meant Crescent City. Because her apartment would be empty without these three guys. Wherever they were was going to be her home now.

Eisheth reached out and popped them out.

When she could breathe again she was on a wraparound porch with a killer view in a place she'd never been before.

Then Eisheth was gone and back with Caleb in the blink of an eye. He shook his head and reached for her. "I really don't like that." He pulled her in for another hug like he couldn't stop touching her.

Next it was Niko and then Xavier. Eisheth came and gave Piper a peck on her cheek. "I'll come back for a visit, I promise."

She pulled him in for a hug before he could teleport. "Thank you again, for everything. Caleb may not like it, but you're welcome here any time. After all," Piper said, smiling back at the scowling alpha. "I'm queen of this pride now."

"That you are, sweetie." Eisheth winked and then disappeared as well.

Then it was just the four of them and Piper stared down at the city below them happily. They were all alive. The alpha who wanted to curse their pride was dead, and her father would be joining her soon so they could start their new life.

"Where's Cat Solo?" she asked.

"I'll go get him," Niko said. "Just stay here for a minute. I don't want you to come inside until I make sure it's been cleaned."

Xavier chuckled and brushed his shoulder against hers as they leaned against the balcony looking out at the ocean. Caleb joined them on her other side. "Do you like it?" he asked.

"The water is breathtaking," she admitted. "It's quiet, and I like that. It suits me."

"It does," Caleb agreed.

"Okay, here's Cat Solo," Niko said. "I think we've come to some kind of understanding."

Piper was so nervous her baby wasn't going to like her anymore now that she was a leopard, but he snuggled right into her arms just like he always did and purred like mad. Then she saw something sparkly dangling from his collar. "What's this?" she asked, adjusting the leather so she could see it better.

"Well," Niko said, shifting awkwardly. "It's the ring we picked out for you."

Then she realized it was a big fat engagement ring. "All three of you picked this out?"

"We did," Caleb said, wrapping his arms around her waist from behind. "While you stayed home and we went out to run errands. I picked out a few and then the other two came and picked from those...but we all decided this worked the best, including your father."

It had a huge diamond in the center but on either side were lapis lazuli stones, just like in the necklace she still wore. Piper felt tears prick her eyes as she fumbled with the string. "Is this why you didn't want me to go inside?" she asked. "How long has Solo been wearing this?"

Xavier laughed and gently took the cat from her arms.

"About a day now, we figured we'd wait until you noticed, but you never did."

She laughed through her tears. "I can't believe he didn't lose it or try to eat it."

"We kept an eye on him," Niko told her. "We wanted it to be a surprise, but I think this worked out better."

Finally they got the ring off the cat and Piper slipped it on. The yellow gold looked perfect against her tan skin and she smiled. "Yes."

"Yes?" Caleb asked, lightly smacking her ass. "Yes to what?"

"Yes to whatever you want," she said. "Mate, wife...yes."

Then they were kissing her again and she was laughing and Solo was meowing in protest at being squished.

"All right, all right, let's go show our mate her new house before this damn cat runs off," Xavier said.

"Are you ready?" Caleb asked, holding out a hand for her.

Xavier went into the house and held the door open for her, waiting patiently. Niko smiled and watched as she took Caleb's hand. "Yes, I'm ready."

Yes, Piper wanted to see the house. But she was ready for what came next too. As long as these three were there – she'd be ready for anything.

EPILOGUE

PIPER

"Are you sure you have to go to work?" Niko muttered, pulling her in closer.

Piper laughed and tried to extricate herself from their arms, but Xavier and Caleb tightened their grip and she was officially stuck. "Guys, I can't be late for my first day at work."

"I still think you should just take some time off and focus on your thesis," Caleb muttered. "You shouldn't be working so hard anyway." He pressed his hand against her belly gently and gave it a little pat.

"Working isn't going to hurt the babies," she told him. But Piper let herself enjoy the way they surrounded her in the giant bed Caleb had specially commissioned after she moved to Crescent City.

Apparently getting claimed and shifting into a leopard pretty much destroyed IUDs to Piper's dismay. She probably wouldn't have noticed except she'd been moody over the last few weeks and the guys swore she smelled weird. None of them had been around a pregnant female so they had no idea what was wrong with her.

One trip to the shifter doctor later and they found out they were having twins. It had been a complete shock and Piper had a hard time figuring out how she was going to get everything done...but, there were fifteen males in the pride who constantly asked her if she would let them watch the babies.

It wasn't something she was used to. Piper only had her father for most of her life. Then these three insanely hot shifters barreled into her life and demanded she make room for them. Luckily they were rather convincing. She couldn't imagine her life without them even though it hadn't been very long.

The most irritating thing about the whole thing was she had to drive to Sacramento now instead of having Eisheth pop her there and back like he was. But he promised once the babies were there he would take her to Egypt to make up for it. And with a demon best friend and an entire pride to look after the kittens, Piper wouldn't be losing out on anything.

She had her new family, her dad, and her career. There really wasn't anything else she could possibly want out of life.

"Piper! Get your butt down here or you're going to be late!"

She laughed and kicked at the bodies surrounding her. "My dad probably wants me to eat something again."

"Good, you should," Xavier mumbled. "If you don't mind we're going to stay here and sleep some more."

Piper stood and grabbed her robe. When she looked back at her mates all three of them were asleep again. She smiled. Sometimes it was hard to believe they were hers. After all they were gorgeous, driven, dedicated, insanely good at sex, and one hundred percent supportive of her. She never thought there would be a guy out there like that, let alone three.

It had only taken a week to get everything settled. Her father had opted to live in the house with them since it was massive. Piper loved being so close to him again, and she'd enjoyed the time off, but she was ready for her first day at the Northern Coastal College library.

Piper quickly got dressed and went downstairs to join her father in the kitchen. He was wearing his new officer's uniform as well and had made sure his schedule matched hers like always.

"I cooked you eggs with lots of onions," her dad said, piling a plate high. "There's sausage and decaf coffee. And no sneaking caffeine at work! It's not good for the babies."

She smiled and sipped the decaf coffee. Her father was so excited to be a grandfather and it was frickin' adorable. "Of course, Dad. I wouldn't dream of it."

"Thanks Papa Smurf!" Eisheth popped in and snatched a sausage off her plate and earned a smack on the hand with the spatula. She loved that her father just put another sausage on her plate. "So it's your first day, nervous?" Eisheth asked.

Piper shook her head and ate. The demon liked to pop in and out randomly to keep her updated on things with the Council and the crocs. After what happened with Forneus and Circe he was extremely invested in shifter affairs, or so he said. With her mates and Eisheth Piper had no doubts they'd find a way to end the blood feud.

"I get to be the demon-father to my niece and nephew, right?" Of course when the demon heard the news he'd made a huge thing out of telling her the sex of the babies like he was some kind of strange, fairy godfather—fairy demonfather?

Her dad choked on his sausage and blustered, but Piper just patted Eisheth's hand. "Of course you can be the demon-father. We're not religious anymore, and the twins will have an entire pride of godfathers so it's totally fine, right Dad?"

Richard Kostopoulos said some very not-nice things in Greek and then Eisheth returned the favor. "I'm getting ready to go, I'll drive you," her dad said, ignoring the demon completely.

When her father left the kitchen with his thermos of coffee she poked Eisheth with her fork. "You really don't need to be so ornery."

"Well, we're all known for something aren't we?" Eisheth adjusted the lapels of his perfect suit and then kissed her on the cheek. "Call me if you need anything. I just wanted to wish you good luck on your first day." And with a little 'pop' he disappeared.

The sound of Xavier roaring made her jump and Piper looked up to see Niko in his leopard form carrying Charlotte in his mouth as a kitten. The little girl didn't even look a little sorry.

"Did she bite X's tail again?" Piper asked.

Niko growled and she took that as a 'yes.' Piper smiled as she grabbed her purse. Niko was going to be an amazing father. She slid off the stool and narrowly avoided Xavier who was being followed by Cat Solo. "Sorry about your tail X."

He sat next to the front door and snorted at her. Solo kept trying to get his tail as it moved back and forth impatiently.

"Yeah, yeah, I'm going to be late," she muttered.

But before she could leave Caleb grabbed her hand and pulled her in for a kiss. "Keep me updated," he murmured. Then he kissed her again, taking his sweet time until her father honked his horn. "I love you."

"I love you too," she said with a smile. Caleb smacked her ass. It made her laugh and she gave Xavier a pat as she walked by which she knew he didn't like, but tolerated for her. Surprisingly Caleb was the one who enjoyed pets in his cat form.

Piper got into her father's cop car and waved goodbye to the other leopards and Niko who still held Charlotte in his mouth. Then she saw one of the Lego droids in her father's cup holders. It made Piper grin as she tucked it into her purse to return to the Falcon later.

There was absolutely nothing she would change about her life.

Don't miss For Fox Sake
A standalone reverse harem shifter book that
takes place in the same paranormal world.

Follow me on Amazon or Bookbub for
updates when it goes live.

Or sign up for my newsletter if you need
updates on the next book!

Want more Reverse Harem?
I have a slow burn reverse harem
space fantasy series – Draga Court
4 books currently live and only two more to go (will be
complete by end of 2018).
A harem member is added every 1-2 books.
But it is still steamy.

Want more Paranormal Shifter Romance?
In the same universe as Spotted Her First
I have a straight MF (male/female)
wolf shifter romance series – Blue Mountain Wolf Pack.

OTHER BOOKS BY EMMA DEAN

Blue Mountain Wolf Pack

Alpha Wolf

Broken Wolf

Wolf Moon

Reverse Harem Shifter Romance*

Spotted Her First

For Fox Sake

All Foxed Up

The Draga Court Series

Princess of Draga

Crown of Draga

Jasmine of Draga

Heir of Draga

Queen of Draga

Fate of Draga

Prequel – Royal Guard of Draga*

*Can be read as a standalone before or after Princess of Draga.

*All paranormal stories are in the same world - the Council of Paranormals.

Want updates on when the books are released and my progress with them?

Sign up for my newsletter @ emmadeanromance.com

ABOUT THE AUTHOR

Emma Dean lives and works in California with her husband and son. She loves romance but needed something different so Draga Court was born. Council of Paranormals was soon to follow when shifters came to life.

With too many stories to write the schedule has been filled through 2019.

When she's not writing she's reading, or spending time with her family.

At least now that she's publishing she has an excuse for not folding the laundry ;-)

Follow her on Social Media or
www.emmadeanromance.com

facebook.com/emmadeanromance

twitter.com/emmadeanromance

instagram.com/crowned_stars_publications

Made in United States
North Haven, CT
17 March 2023

34215112R00150